The Guest is History

A MINERVA BIGGS MYSTERY

CORDELIA ROOK

D1520339

.

Chapter One

I COULD'VE TOLD you there were old family secrets buried at Tybryd. I just wouldn't have known I meant it literally.

The thing with skeletons is, they never stay buried forever. One way or another, they always find their way to the surface. The ghost of Edith Cotswold Baird was an especially restless one, reaching out from beyond her unmarked, unknown grave to cause another murder, more than a century after her own. I'm sure that wasn't her intention—or maybe it was, who knows—but that's how it happened.

I was not, obviously, murdered in the course of dealing with the whole Edith carriwitchet, which was nice for me. Mine was just one of the many lives she wreaked her special brand of havoc on. No, that's not fair: of course the real havoc-wreaker was her killer.

On the January day that brought the modern wave of said havoc, I was less than two months into my perfect new job, running the dog daycare at the Tybryd hotel and resort. The daycare had been my idea; calling it Tailbryd had been my boyfriend (and boss) Percy's. I'm sure we can all agree Tailbryd is a hideous name. The worst of all worlds, really, cutesy without being cute. But I'd been happy to go along if it meant Percy would go along with the rest. Besides, it made him smile, which meant I got the dimples. There was always value in the dimples.

My pitch, delivered the summer before, had been simple: Tybryd had always been officially dog friendly, but in practice, guests rarely brought their dogs with them. A lot of them might have loved having their furry friends along on hikes and other outdoor activities, but they did not love leaving those friends alone in strange hotel rooms while they did things like eat fine meals and get spa treatments—things people did tend to do when vacationing at a luxury resort.

And speaking of spa treatments, Tybryd had zero amenities for dogs. So why not build a kennel, I said, not for boarding them overnight (although we would definitely have evening hours), but for keeping them for a few hours here and there? We could even add a grooming salon, so little Zoe and Max could have their nails done while their owners did the same.

Percy and his sister Elaine, who ran their famous family estate together, had both loved the idea. He tacked on his little mashup of *tails* and *Tybryd*, because Percy Baird had never met a dad joke he didn't love, and we were off and running. By Halloween I'd officially left my job in the Events office and had new business cards printed up: *Minerva Biggs, Director of Canine Services*. By Thanksgiving I was presiding over a freshly renovated, state-of-the-art canine resort at the site of one of Tybryd's original stables.

Which was where I was that morning, foolishly thinking Mrs. Horan and her obnoxious terrier mix Jellypie were going to be the lowlight of that day. I remember we had a hard frost the night before, because I was worried the ground might be too cold for the tree guy to do his thing. It wasn't, but I didn't know a lot about tree removal. All I knew was that the prior weekend's storm had brought a big old tree down on the fence of Yard C, and we weren't going to be able to use that yard until the tree guy got the tree out of there, which for reasons beyond my ken involved some amount of digging.

The fact that Yard C was indisposed was a source of some anxiety to Mrs. Horan. "But you've still got the space to separate them into playgroups, right?" she asked me, her small, deep-set eyes regarding my dog Plantagenet with suspicion. "I don't want my sweet little Jellypie thrown in with that pit bull."

I distinctly heard a snicker from Ned Phelps. He was the one who'd called me (and therefore Plant) out of the office to speak with Mrs. Horan, after she'd declared him too young and therefore not senior enough to receive her instructions as to the exact temperature at which Jellypie's lunch must be served. Or, it seemed, to explain to her that the existence of a Yard C implied the coexistence of a Yard A and a Yard B.

He made a hasty retreat, apparently because trying to smother his laugh wasn't working out. The hallway door, which usually did a good job of keeping barks and other noises out of the lobby, hadn't closed all the way before I heard him burst out laughing for real.

Ned knew how people calling Plant a pit bull set me off. At a hundred pounds, Plant was much too big for a pit, and as far as I recalled, I'd never seen a black pit, either. But people did tend to make assumptions about any dog with a square head. Not that it would have been a bad thing if he were a pit bull anyway, but I wasn't enjoying Mrs. Horan's company so much that I relished the idea of sharing a can of worms with her.

"He's not a pit bull." I tried not to sound short about it, but between her comment hitting my pet peeve (pun intended) and her sickly floral perfume giving me a headache, it wasn't easy. "But as I think Ned was explaining, we assign the dogs to groups by energy level, play style, and size. Being that granular about it is the reason we have three yards, even though we rarely have enough dogs at any given time to use them all."

"What group is Jellypie going to be in?" she wanted to know. "Are there any dachshunds in it? Jellypie does not like dachshunds."

This information failed to shock me. In my admittedly brief acquaintance with Jellypie, I hadn't known her to like much of anybody. She'd already yapped at Plant so many times I'd had to move him out of her line of sight. "I don't believe there are any dachshunds in today, but if we find she's not comfortable with other dogs, she'll get some solo playtime with one of our staff instead."

"She's fine with other dogs," Mrs. Horan said, despite having just warned me to keep her dog away from every dachshund on the planet. "She hasn't got a mean bone in her body. But it's probably best if she just has one-on-one time anyway." She hugged Jellypie closer and made smooching noises over her head. "She prefers to be the center of attention, don't you, Jelly-Welly-Bear?"

Also not a surprise. "Solo dogs do incur a higher hourly rate."

I was expecting an argument, but Mrs. Horan waved that away. "Nothing is too expensive for my Jellykins."

Despite the recent drastic increase in my exposure to other people's dogs, I continued to be amazed by the vazey things they called them. But as Percy was fond of pointing out, I wasn't exactly qualified to judge, considering I had an animal I called Plant.

Mrs. Horan had exhausted her extensive list of requirements, and I was about to take possession of Jelly-Welly-Bear at last, when Ned came rushing back to the front desk. I could tell by his face—even paler than usual, putting his many freckles in sharp relief—that something was very wrong.

He didn't really say anything. Just sort of squeaked something that might have involved the phrase *need a word*.

My heart started to pound. Outside of laughing at ridiculous people and their spoiled dogs, Ned was pretty unflappable. Whatever it was, it had to be bad.

I excused myself from Mrs. Horan and called for somebody else to take Jellypie to her kennel instead, then pulled Ned into my small office. When I say small, I mean small—my desk and Plant's bed took up most of it. But it had the benefit of a door, which I now made use of to shut out the sound of Mrs. Horan beginning her list of instructions again, this time to poor Taren Miller. Plant, indifferent to both the close quarters and my anxiety, pushed past Ned to curl up on the bed.

"What happened?" I asked. "It's not Bailey is it, because I told—"

"It's not Bailey," said Ned. "It's ... the tree guy, Mike?"

I frowned. "Tell me he did not cut the fiber cable or something. Is the internet down?"

"Uh ..." Ned swallowed. "Nooooo. But I think this is worse."

"Out with it, then."

"He found bones."

"Sorry, did you just say bones?" Probably justifiably, considering my surroundings and my new occupation, my mind immediately went to dogs and that cliché about them burying bones. I was completely bewildered.

Then I realized what he must mean. "Like, *human* bones?"

"Like a dead body," Ned said.

Well, thank goodness for that. When I'd first seen him looking so blanched and terrified, I was afraid a dog had died.

Chapter Two

PERCY and I leaned against the fence of Yard C, assuring Officer Roark McGinty that we hadn't killed anybody and buried their body near the old stable lately. Or earlier than lately, I guessed, if the body was already down to just bones.

I doubted Roark actually needed much assurance on that front; he was friendly with both of us. But we had to give some sort of statement, considering Tybryd was Percy's property and Tailbryd was my responsibility. And since we still had no idea what was going on, *We didn't do it* was pretty much all we had.

We'd been out there at least an hour. Ruby Walker, the chief of Bryd Hollow's police department, and the county medical examiner were partially hidden behind the remains of the fallen oak that had started all this mess. Roark was tasked with managing the crowd, which now consisted of only Percy and me. Ned and Taren had long since gone back inside to tend to the dogs. Plant, thoroughly disgruntled after being told several times that he was not needed to inspect the bones himself, had gone with them in a huff.

I didn't blame any of them. The temperature wasn't so bad, but the wind was cutting right through my coat. Percy caught me shivering and pulled me closer, my back against his broad chest, so he could wrap his arms around me.

"Minerva could probably wait inside, couldn't she?" he asked Roark.

I snorted before Roark could answer. "Good luck with that. I need to know what's going on just as much as you do."

"Yeah," said Percy, "but I'm so much tougher than you are."

I gave his foot a little stomp, not hard enough to hurt or anything, just hard enough so he'd know he wasn't funny. He was warm though, I'd give him that. And he smelled awfully good.

Ruby finally came to talk to us, and maybe I was imagining things, but I thought her sigh sounded almost … bored. Maybe there wasn't much of a case here for her, after all. Maybe the tree guy had been mistaken, and they'd actually been animal bones. A girl could hope.

"All right," she said, then pursed her lips. Ruby Walker specialized in neon-bright glasses that stood out sharply against her warm brown skin, the better to draw your eye when she lowered them to glare disapprovingly from over the top. This season she'd swapped out her usual teal for a brilliant lime, but the effect was still the same as she settled that stern look on Percy, as if to express her disappointment that he'd interrupted her day by having ground with bones in it. "Here's the summary. Your tree service found the skeleton of a female—I don't have an age on her yet, you'll have to wait on that—who was buried quite some time ago."

"What does 'quite some time' mean?" asked Roark. He sounded mildly annoyed, like he too was beginning to suspect that he'd been standing out in the cold for no good reason.

"The ME needs more time to examine the remains," said Ruby, "but she thinks this woman probably died a century ago. The condition of the skull suggests blunt force trauma to the head. So either she was murdered or she had a nasty accident. Most likely Door Number One, considering there's no casket or any of the other things we associate with a formal burial. I don't think there was ever a family plot here at Tybryd anyway, was there?"

She'd directed the question to Percy, but I answered for him. Of the two of us, I was more familiar with the estate's—and his family's—history than he was. "No, the only family plot is at St. Asaph's."

Ruby held up an evidence bag. "She did have some things on her, though. Minerva, you might as well look at these too, they're probably more your department than Percy's."

She didn't bother putting on gloves before pulling three objects out of the bag. I supposed there wasn't going to be much processing of this evidence. I didn't know whether it was possible for fingerprints to survive after so long in the ground, but even if there were any, there hadn't exactly been fingerprint databases to match them against a hundred years ago.

Besides, whoever had killed our mystery woman would be long dead themselves. Would there even be an investigation, once they confirmed the skeleton's age for sure? Or would she be without justice forever? Haunting Tybryd, probably, now that her bones had been disturbed. Well, she could just get in line and wait her turn. There were plenty of restless spirits here already, if the ghost tour was to be believed. The resort had been the Baird family's private residence until the 1950s, and some of them had led eventful—and maybe a tad bit murderous—lives.

The first thing Ruby showed us was a medallion on a chain, both of them silver and too tarnished to see very well. I thought the medallion might have some sort of animal on it. It struck me as a little on the big side for a piece of women's jewelry, but the second thing, a plain gold wedding band, looked appropriately sized for a woman's finger.

The final item was a gold pocket watch, definitely expensive back then, and much more so now that it was an antique. And definitely a man's.

"You're sure this was a woman?" I asked.

"The ME is positive," Ruby said.

"Huh." I looked again at the watch and the medallion.

"I always wondered how they could tell," said Percy. Since he'd never expressed any interest in the gender identification of skeletons before, I assumed it was his polite way of expressing the same skepticism I was.

"There are a few ways," Roark offered. "Pelvis, skull.

There are anatomical differences even in bones. And she'll have taken some measurements."

All right, then. I supposed we could trust that the professional medical examiner was better at this than we were. So why had this woman been wearing men's accessories when she died?

Ruby opened the watch and held it out between me and Percy. "You can take it. We've cleaned it off, and you can see the engraving there."

Percy took it and leaned toward me so I could look at the same time. I was hoping for some long, sentimental message that would give us some clues, but there were only three letters: *RRB*.

RRB. Why did that seem familiar? I assumed they were initials. And given where we were standing, the *B* must be for *Baird*. I scanned my mental image of the Baird family tree.

Oh. Right. But that can't ...
Odsbodikins.

"You said a century, right?" I asked Ruby. I waited for her nod before turning to Percy. "Have you called your mother yet?"

"No."

"Call her."

Mrs. B was the keeper of family lore, mostly passed down from her mother-in-law, who'd probably gotten it from her mother-in-law. If I married Percy, that task would fall to me as the history person of the next generation. (I had a degree in it, and once taught high-school history.) Not that we were talking marriage yet, other than the occasional vague reference to the future. We'd been together ten months, give or take, and were now in that slightly awkward phase where the words *boyfriend* and *girlfriend* don't quite cut it, but you're not engaged either.

I was sure we were heading in that direction. And I was sure he felt the same way. Mostly sure. Usually. But marriage was a big change, and marrying into Old Money was an even bigger one. I was perfectly fine with letting things unfold in their own time. Mostly fine. Usually.

Anyway, that lore task already had fallen to me, in some ways; I'd recently taken on the gargantuan project of scanning and cataloging all the old Baird family photos. But I was going to need Mrs. B's superior expertise for this.

Percy took out his phone and started tapping at it, texting rather than calling. "Okay, but in the meanwhile you might as well tell us what's up. I know that look in your eye, and I imagine Ruby's seen it a time or two herself."

Ruby snorted. "The look like she's about to start telling me how to do my job, you mean?"

He looked up at her. "Is it your job, if this turns out to be as old as you think? Would you really investigate?"

She waggled her hand. "Not very hard, I can tell you that. And I wouldn't be waiting with bated breath on any lab results, either. Nobody's got the staff or the time to spend on a case that's a hundred years old."

"Well then, there you go." Percy grinned at me. He was in a pretty good mood, I noticed, now that the dead person on his property turned out not to have been murdered on his watch. Not that I blamed him, considering Tybryd was his livelihood. And pretty much his whole world, unless you wanted to count me and Plant. Who were pretty much part of Tybryd at this point anyway. "It can be Minerva's job."

I voiced no agreement, but I didn't argue the point, either. Where Ruby's interest ended, mine began. Century-old skeletons were exactly my thing. As for the murder part, Percy usually discouraged my investigative tendencies, but I guessed he figured it had to be safe if the murderer was definitely dead.

"So what does the engraving mean to you?" he asked.

"They're Roderick Baird's initials," I said. "He was Roderick Robert Baird."

I'd expected Ruby's blank look, but I shook my head at Percy, who obviously didn't recognize the name any more than she did. This was one of his relatives we were talking about, if a distant one. And it wasn't like the guy didn't have a claim to family fame. "He died on the *Titanic*, Percy, jeez."

This didn't seem to carry quite the same weight with him as it did with me. "Then it's probably not his," he said with a shrug. "You'd think his watch would be at the bottom of the North Atlantic."

"At least you know where the ship sank."

"I saw the movie."

Ruby took the watch from him, and dropped it back into the bag with the medallion and the ring. "I'm going to take this stuff for now, but I doubt I'll keep it long. I can't use it for much."

She gestured back at Yard C and the turned earth

beyond. "Same with this. We took some soil samples, in case anyone wants them, but other than that I'm not calling this a crime scene or anything. You're free to finish your tree work and get back to normal."

Percy ran his hand through his dark hair, and blew out a slow sigh of relief. But I wondered what kind of "normal" I was expected to find, when I'd just been delivered some twentieth-century bones and a mysterious connection to the *Titanic*. The bones would've captured my attention either way, but truth be told, I was a bit of a *Titanic* nerd. I was honest with myself: I wasn't going to be sparing any excess thought for Jellypie anytime soon.

We said our goodbyes to Ruby, and Percy put his arm around me to warm me up as we walked inside. "You heard the woman," he said. "For once, you've got a murder all to yourself."

And I did, for a little while. Until the second murder, anyway.

Chapter Three

"Oh, that is *definitely* Roddy Baird's watch!"

Mrs. B—everybody called Bessie Baird *Mrs. B*, even, on occasion, her children— always spoke in exclamations and italics. But this was a bold statement even for her, considering she hadn't even seen the watch.

I was kicking myself for not asking Ruby if I could take a couple of pictures before she took Skeleton Lady's things away. She'd probably have smacked me upside the head if I asked such a question about a modern-day murder, but she didn't seem too concerned about the sanctity of this particular evidence. She also seemed to think she'd be returning the items to the Bairds fairly quickly; I would make sure I got some pictures then, but in the meanwhile, Mrs. B was flying blind.

Plant and I were having dinner with Percy and Mrs. B at Baird House. It was a little more weird that Percy lived with his mother now that he was the only sibling left in the house, but it was a lot less weird than you'd think your thirty-one-year-old boyfriend living with his

15

mom would be. It was different when your mom's house was a historic mansion (originally built for a Baird dowager who was, by reputation, actually not the sort of relative you wanted living a mile away). And it was family tradition for the children to stay until they had a family of their own. The house would be passed on to one of them upon their marriage, and the cycle would begin again.

Usually it was one of the older siblings who got it, but none of them wanted it. That left Percy holding the bag, even though he was the youngest. Or holding the mansion. Which wasn't such a terrible thing to hold. Will the last one leaving Baird House please take the keys.

When Percy got married, Mrs. B would probably move out before the wedding cake was served. But until then, she was still the mistress of the manor, commanding the head of the table and our full attention. "That's Roddy's watch," she said again, "and that's his wife Edith's skeleton."

"You sound pretty sure," I said.

"Of course I'm sure! The story is *legend*! It was a *very* big deal, especially since it ended here at Tybryd. I'm surprised neither of you has ever heard about it, honestly."

Percy pointed at his mother. "That would be your fault. Who would we have heard it from, if not you?"

"I don't know, Minerva just always seems to"—Mrs. B waved her fork in my direction—"*know* things."

"I know Roderick went down on the *Titanic*," I said, "although apparently his watch did not. And I know he was Alistair's nephew, his oldest brother's son. And that's about all I know." Alistair Baird was the founder of Tybryd and the Baird dynasty as I—and America—knew it. His brother's branch of the family were still Bairds, obviously, and wealthy in their own right, but I imagined as far as Roderick's contemporaries were concerned, he wasn't really one of *them*.

Mrs. B gestured at me with her empty wine glass before reaching for the bottle. "No, his watch did *not* go down with him. We already *knew* that."

Percy cocked his head at her. "We did?"

"We *did*." She gave herself a pretty generous pour. Maybe we were in for a long story. Or maybe she was just excited to tell it. She really was deeply into the family history; it was the main thing she and I had bonded over.

Either way, I was more than game. Dante—the Bairds' personal chef—had made fried chicken, so as far as I was concerned, I had nothing but time. I took another thigh from the platter and sat back to wait for Mrs. B to enlighten us.

"Roddy was a youngish man," she said, "maybe thirty, and off gallivanting around Europe. Then one day, out of the blue, his family gets a telegram. It says he's married an Englishwoman he met in Italy, and that her name is Edith Cotswold. And that's *all* it says. Because, you know, it's a *telegram*."

"They could send telegrams across the ocean?" Percy looked at me for confirmation. I settled for a simple nod rather than delivering a treatise on trans-Atlantic telegraph cables, which I thought showed admirable restraint.

"I know the next part," I said. "*Titanic* has been sort

of a morbid hobby of mine. Roderick and Edith were sailing home when the disaster struck. He asked the crew if he could get on the lifeboat with her, because she was pregnant."

"Was she really pregnant?" Percy asked. "Or was he just saying that because it worked for JJ Astor?"

"It didn't work for JJ Astor. He died." I passed a tiny bite of chicken to Plant, who was resting his chin on my knee, patiently awaiting his share. I knew a lot of people were horrified by feeding dogs from the table, but as none of those people were at that particular table, their opinions didn't really count. "And it didn't work for Roderick either. They told him no men were being loaded onto the boats until all the women and children were. So he died, and Edith made it home."

"But you're missing the crucial part!" said Mrs. B. "Well, crucial for our purposes today. It was while they were saying goodbye on deck, just before she got into the lifeboat and never saw him again, that he gave her his watch. As a token of his love, and to bring back to his family, so they would know his dying wish was that they take care of her and the Baird baby she was carrying."

She sighed as she took another sip of wine. "So *romantic*. They say she always carried it with her, from that day forward. The way I heard it was that she carried it for luck, but *that* can't be right, can it? It wasn't exactly lucky for Roddy, was it?"

"Was it lucky for her, is the question." Percy pushed his now empty plate away from him and leaned forward on crossed forearms. "Did the family honor his wish, and take care of her and the baby?"

"Yes, they did," said Mrs. B.

"Not very well, apparently," I said. "Assuming that was her we found today."

Mrs. B raised her glass in acknowledgment of the point. "You're right, and it definitely *was* her. Not only because the watch was buried with her, but because Edith was here for the midsummer party in 1913. She brought Roddy's little son with her. He wasn't even a year old." She smacked her hand against the table. "And Edith *disappeared from that party*."

The dramatic ending to Mrs. B's tale—or what I mistook for the ending—had its intended effect on me. I stared at her. "That might be part of the family legend, but I guess they hushed it up pretty well from the public. I've never seen it written anywhere or anything."

"'The Midsummer Party of 1913?" Percy laughed. "You make it sound like it was a famous thing. Like the War of 1812."

I shook my head. "Not a famous thing, a regular one. Before the annual ball, there was the annual midsummer party. One of those week-long house party type things rich people used to do. Mostly in Newport, but Alistair and Emily liked to be special."

Percy drummed his fingers against the table, eyeing me with what I hoped was feigned suspicion. "I can't decide whether it's endearing that you know this much about my family, or if I should get a restraining order. It's a little creepy, if you want the truth."

"I don't know about it because of *you*. I know about it because Emily took photographs." I gave Mrs. B a pointed look. "This is on you, you know, for raising him to think he's the center of everything."

She patted her son's shoulder. "Well, he should be."

"Okay, so Edith comes to this famous regular house party and then just"—Percy made a *poof* motion with his hands—"disappears? They never found out what happened to her?"

"They thought they *knew* what happened to her," said Mrs. B. "Nobody thought she *died*. If you'd asked me for this story a week ago, I would have told you what I was told: that she had an affair, stole some jewelry, and ran away."

"Hold on, stole some jewelry?" I asked.

Mrs. B nodded. "Several of Emily's pieces, and a few of the guests', went missing at the same time. And Edith was seen with a *man*. A couple of times that week, skulking around at night. A *stranger*."

Sure she was. A stranger who'd murdered her, buried her out by the stable, and stole some stuff on his way out. You didn't need to find her body to at least see that possibility. "She had a son," I said, "a *baby* son, and everybody just assumed she'd left him behind? And why would she steal jewelry? Didn't she have Roderick's money?"

Mrs. B put her hand over mine. "You can *always* use more money, dear."

"So that's it? Nobody even looked for her? Or even entertained the idea of foul play?" I was more than a little offended on Edith's behalf.

Apparently Mrs. B felt no such sisterhood with this wronged Baird wife. She only shrugged. "Nobody liked Edith very much, so I suppose it was easy to think the worst of her. *My* mother-in-law heard from *her* mother-in-law, who knew Edith *personally*, that Edith was a big —well, you know."

We did know, or at least we got the idea, but that didn't stop Mrs. B from spelling it out—literally. She put her hand to the side of her mouth and loudly whispered, "*Witch with a B.*" Then she giggled at her own naughtiness. Maybe it was time to cut her off.

Percy and I carefully avoided eye contact, lest we burst out laughing in the poor woman's face. Instead he looked down at the table, spinning his fork in slow circles. "So if Edith had a son, is that branch of the family still around? If one of them will do a DNA test, that'd be the easiest way to identify the bones, right? And we'll want to give them the watch and stuff."

I nodded. "That watch will be worth thousands. Probably a lot of them."

Now he did look at me, and it was a skeptical look. "You think?"

"Don't underestimate how much genuine *Titanic* artifacts go for," I said. "It wasn't recovered from the wreckage, obviously, but it was on the ship, belonged to somebody who died there, and was brought back by a survivor. And *Titanic* people can be really weird."

He snickered. "Yes, you can be."

Mrs. B snapped her fingers, as if something had just come to her. "Barbara Hingley! That's her name. Your father heard from her every now and then, and I still get a Christmas card from her. I think. And her daughter, too. Kim something?"

"Have you ever met them?" Percy asked.

"Not a once. But I'll get in touch with Barbara and let her know what happened." Mrs. B sighed. "Although I'm not sure how I'll do that. We don't *know* what happened, do we?"

"No, we don't." Percy flashed me the dimples. "But Min says she's going to find out."

"I never said that!" I protested. Not out loud, anyway.

But I was totally, definitely going to find out.

Chapter Four

EMILY BAIRD—ALISTAIR'S wife—had been ahead of her time, as far as being that person (usually a mom) at every event who wants a picture of everything. She'd had a lot of photographs taken, including group photos from every midsummer house party, Baird ball, and other occasion she hosted. Most of these now resided in Baird House's top attic, along with (as far as I could tell) two other generations of Baird photos, usually labeled, sometimes not, and with no discernible attempt at organization.

When I'd suggested to Mrs. B that she should preserve them all digitally, she'd duly bought the best photo scanner on the market and told me I'd best get started right away, because she'd like the project to be completed by next year's ball. She'd changed that instruction slightly at dinner the other night: she wanted me to find the photo from the 1913 midsummer party as soon as possible, as Edith Baird was bound to be in it.

Bless her heart, the woman genuinely tried not to

treat people like servants—when she remembered to. She would not tolerate the use of what she deemed *servant words* in her house; my friend Snick was the household manager, never the butler. And she'd certainly done a good job of raising her children not to be snobs, going so far as to insist they attend the local public schools. (This hadn't kept any of them from the ivy league, not even Tristan, who'd dropped out after two years.) Elaine had even married a townie.

But history and local culture worked against Mrs. B on this one. The town of Bryd Hollow had been founded in service of Tybryd, and all these years later not much had changed. Nearly every resident of working age either worked at Tybryd, had a spouse who worked at Tybryd, or owned a local business that served Tybryd's guests and employees. In other words, the town was still populated by servants. It was easy, I supposed, to forget you weren't a feudal lord when you practically lived in a fiefdom.

And doubly so when it came to me, since at one time I actually had been her servant; I'd come here in the first place as the family's personal assistant. After her husband died, Mrs. B decided they didn't need a PA anymore, and never replaced me in that role. But she still occasionally seemed to expect me to fill it.

So there I was, spending my Saturday afternoon in the enormous yet somehow stuffy attic, surrounded by a century's worth of detritus. Not that I really minded. I hadn't resisted Mrs. B when she assigned me the job because I would have volunteered for it if she hadn't. One man's detritus was my treasure, provided it was old enough to qualify as history.

Plant didn't mind too much, either. I'd cleared the floor where the center front window made a sun spot, and put a fluffy blanket down for him. He was as content to nap there as anywhere.

Whoever had moved all the old things from Tybryd to Baird House when the former was converted to a hotel hadn't seemed to have any concept of, say, categories. There weren't boxes of photos, per se. There were just ... boxes. And trunks. And crates and cartons and cases. Hats packed away with silver cutlery. Old books with carefully wrapped crystal glasses. Photographs ranging from the 1900s to the 1950s tossed pretty much anywhere and everywhere, tucked into empty spaces between jewelry and teacups and scarves.

Considering what I had to work with, it was easier for me to do that work here, unpleasant as this attic was (I'd once been shot in it), than to take things back and forth between Baird House and my apartment. Thankfully somebody had run electricity up here at some point. The photo scanner and my laptop were set up on an old table in the corner.

Usually the photographs had at least a year written on the back, if not an exact date or description. Many of these were traced over or scrawled anew in Mrs. B's mother-in-law's hand, suggesting she'd at some point gone through the pictures, probably when she was looking for specific ones she wanted to frame for display, and then just left them where they were. I couldn't bear to do such a half-hearted job of it, and was doing my best to be as systematic as possible. I scanned each photo I found, made notes in the electronic file, then filed the paper photo away according to year in the new filing cabinet Mrs. B had bought for that purpose.

It was taking forever.

Which was fine under ordinary circumstances, but now I was in a hurry. I'd been thinking about Edith Cotswold Baird and little else for three days. I'd gotten a little obsessive, if you want the whole truth. And I really wanted to see her face.

Not to mention, if Edith had been murdered at the midsummer party that year, then my top suspects were the alleged mysterious stranger, who may or may not have been a fabrication to cover the real killer's tracks, and the other people there. I needed to know who they were. As far as I knew, no guest lists from those parties had survived. I would just have to use the photograph to try to match names to faces.

Several records searches had already told me that Edith was born in England to a family of means, but not so many means that they were aristocrats, and had two sisters and one brother who survived to adulthood with her. She married Roderick Baird in Italy at the age of twenty-one, and not long afterward returned to England with him to board the *Titanic* at Southhampton. I'd found her name and Roderick's on the list of first-class passengers, hers with a letter *S* for *Survived* beside it, his with a cross for the tragic alternative.

I'd also once again borrowed Emily Baird's journals from Mrs. B. The volumes weren't dated, but I knew from experience which one encompassed 1913. Emily rarely said anything directly, and it wasn't always easy to crack her code, but I found some sketches (Emily Baird was a prolific sketcher) and a bit of rambling text that suggested the events of the midsummer party. Unfortunately, they didn't tell me anything I hadn't already heard from Mrs. B. If Emily had any strong feelings about Edith Baird—such as outrage over her missing jewels, for example—she hadn't recorded them for posterity.

What I hadn't found—so far—was a single picture of Edith, anywhere. If any photos were taken at her and Roderick's wedding, they hadn't survived the sinking of the *Titanic*. I'd even tracked down the names of some descendants of Edith's siblings, in hopes that there might be an old family photo on their side. But trying to find the right Mary Cotswold and Jane-Ann Weaver among all the many Mary Cotswolds and Jane Weavers on social media was slow going. Most people didn't even reply to a stranger asking questions.

So I still had no face to match to Edith's name—or to her bones. But surely that was about to change. I decided I could buck my thorough-but-slow-as-molasses system for one day, and started piling photographs up by the table rather than scanning them right away.

I was sitting on the floor in front of an old-fashioned milk crate, overturned to serve as a makeshift desk, going through yet another stack of photos when Plant's head snapped up, tail thumping against his blanket. A second later I heard Percy call my name as he clambered up the squeaking and groaning old staircase. I stood and kissed his cheek as he came in.

"I didn't know you were doing this today." He gave me a longer, more interesting kiss on the lips, but it was ended abruptly when an impatient Plant tried his best to tackle him.

"Plant!" I snapped. "Off! *Sit!*"

Plant did as he was told, but not without sending a very judgy and resentful look my way. Hand to my heart, that dog poked out his lower lip when he pouted, like a small child.

Percy reached down to give him some consolation scritches. "I would've helped you."

"Helped me with the pictures, or helped Plant with the misbehaving?" I asked.

"Well, either." He put his hands in his pockets and rocked back on his heels. "Definitely the misbehaving, at a minimum. But I was talking to you."

"You had your male bonding thing." He'd gone to Asheville for a brewery tour with Elaine's husband Phil. "How was it? I didn't think you'd be back so early."

"It's not early."

I looked at my phone. It was not, in fact, early. It seemed I'd completely lost track of time. I'd have to go back to my apartment and shower soon; we had dinner plans with our friends Paul and Carrie.

And I'd missed a couple of texts. "Did you see this message from your mother?"

"Yep, and I just talked to her."

The text, to both Percy and me, said she'd talked to Barbara Hingley, and that both Barbara and her daughter Kim Hollander were coming next Saturday to stay for a week, and would we please arrange nice rooms for them at Tybryd?

I looked up at Percy. "They're coming here? Why?"

"Brave of them, isn't it, considering the last time one of them came to Tybryd we murdered her and then trashed her reputation to cover it up." He chuckled at his own joke. "Sounds like they bullied my mom into an invitation. She said Barbara's a real"—he lowered his voice to a stage whisper—"*witch with a B*."

I laughed. "Tell me she hasn't been drinking at four o'clock in the afternoon."

"Nah, she didn't say it exactly like that. But that was the gist. I guess Barbara just wants to come see where the bones were found, and I don't know, ask some questions, shake her fist a little. Demand justice be served. I'll be sure to let her know you're the one to talk to for that."

"Ha ha. Wouldn't it be better to wait on all that until we've confirmed for sure that it's Edith?" They'd be helping with that, I assumed, and of course they would want Edith's things. But as far as I knew, there was no rule that said either DNA samples or watches must be collected from within the walls of luxury resorts.

Percy waved the practicality (or lack thereof) away, confirming my suspicion that the visit wasn't entirely about Edith. "Sounds like it's just an excuse to get a free stay at Tybryd. My mother says Barbara's got a huge chip on her shoulder about being a real Baird, and being treated like an outsider or whatever. When she was younger she was always angling for invitations to the ball and stuff."

"So why didn't your parents just invite her?"

He shrugged. "Because petty spite was my father's primary hobby? I imagine it amused him to shun her."

Fair enough. Clifford Baird had been a cruel man. It

was a credit to Mrs. B that all his children turned out to be nice people.

"But speaking of confirming it's Edith," Percy said, "Barbara is sending the county a DNA sample. She'd be Edith's granddaughter, and apparently there's such a thing as a grandparent test, specifically. I don't know if it's a hundred percent, but it sounds like it's pretty good, and it'll at least confirm a biological relationship. In the meanwhile, she's got something else that might help. Some old book she says was Edith's. Passed on to her from her father."

"What kind of book?" I asked. "How would that help?"

"She didn't say what kind, but it's got a leather cover with a bear inside a circle of leaves on it."

"Ah." Ruby had already turned the watch, necklace, and ring over to Mrs. B, since they were found on Baird property. Once the silver medallion was cleaned, it was plain that the image stamped on it was a bear, inside a circle of what looked like ash leaves. I already knew the symbol was at least somewhat unusual, because I'd asked around about it and hadn't found anybody who recognized it. I didn't know if that was enough to prove the necklace's wearer to be the same person who owned the book, but it would at least support that conclusion. Especially with all the other evidence we had to suggest the bones were Edith's.

"Anyway, Barbara's going to bring it with her," said Percy. "I don't know why she's so anxious for us to believe it's Edith, when she could just wait for science to confirm it for her. Maybe she thinks we won't turn the stuff over to her otherwise."

I frowned. "That's ridiculous, of course you will. The watch is definitely Roderick's, regardless, so that's rightfully hers either way. And that's the only thing with any real monetary value."

"Yeah, and apparently she's already looking to cash in. She asked my mom to put her in touch with anybody who might want to buy it."

"That was fast. So much for sentimental value, I g— Plant, will you stop?"

Plant, once again impatient at not being the center of Percy's attention, had dragged his blanket over, violently wiggling his entire body like some sort of giant, deranged worm. Showing people cloth items—blankets, napkins, their own sweaters—was a great joy of Plant's.

Percy knew his part. "That is *so nice*! What a lucky dog you are, to have such a nice blanket!" He sounded a bit like his mother.

This of course made Plant prance and wiggle all the more. And the thing with Plant was, he had a tail any iguana would envy. That thing could break a nose, if you were foolish enough to sit too close to him in full wag. Everything around him was in danger, a fact I knew well.

"Plant, settle down," I warned.

Too late. His tail banged against the milk crate and swept the stack of photos I'd been going through off it. Then he backed into it, knocking the whole thing over. I threw myself to the floor like a Secret Service agent protecting the President, ready to defend the photographs against being trod on by his big dumb feet.

Percy grabbed Plant's collar, recovered the blanket, and spread it back out on the floor. "Why don't you sit for a bit, friend." Plant sat, still looking very proud.

I could've picked up all the photos by then, but instead I was lying on the dusty floor (I really was going to need that shower), clutching one of them in my hand.

"Plant, you're a genius!" I sat up to give my dog a kiss on the head, then stood to show Percy what I—well, Plant—had found. "This is it!"

"Are you sure?"

I was. I'd seen a few midsummer party photographs from other years, and I could tell by the east garden location, the size of the group, and their clothing that this was one of them. The year *1913* was written in faint pencil on the back.

The dimples came out as Percy leaned in for a closer look. As always, the smell of his soap was divine. I would have liked to kiss him again, but I wasn't willing to risk further canine interference, especially with the photograph in my hand.

"So which one is Edith?" he asked.

Which one, indeed. Of the sixteen people pictured, all were adults. If children had been invited to these parties, they were never included in the photographs. The subjects were arranged by height, rather than grouped by couples or families, so that was no help. Nine of them were women.

"I don't know." I gently tapped one of the women's faces. "But that's Emily Baird."

Another tap. "That's Constance," I said, referring to Emily and Alistair's daughter.

Then one final tap. "And this one is George's wife. Or I guess she was probably his fiancée then. Or maybe even just a hopeful friend."

Percy laughed. *"Hopeful friend?"*

"I don't know, I don't remember what year they got married." I cleared my throat. I had no idea where that turn of phrase had come from, but it had struck me too. And not in a good way. Thank heavens for the low light; maybe he wouldn't see me blushing, and ask why I was being weird.

Was that how he saw me? Or how his family did? Was *I* a hopeful friend?

I did not want to be a hopeful friend.

Odsbodikins, Minerva, my inner voice lectured. *You're a grown-up. Supposedly. You could just ask him if he's thinking marriage.*

See, but the thing with asking questions is, he tends to answer them, I countered. *What if I don't like the answer?*

"So, um ..." I coughed again. "That leaves six. Once I get it scanned I can do some manipulation and enhancement. That should help."

Percy gave the picture a couple of taps of his own. "Don't need to enhance it to see those two are too old to be Edith."

"Right. Good eye." So that left four. And now I was going to meet Edith's granddaughter and great-granddaughter. Maybe they would look like somebody in the photo.

My awkward moment was forgotten as I stared at the photograph, prickling with the kind of excitement only historical research could make me feel. (I assume it's already been clearly established, and need not be repeated here, that I was a nerdy weirdo.)

Where was she? Where was this woman who, like me, had come to these mountains in search of a fresh start, a new home, maybe even a family of her own?

I sure hoped it would work out better for me.

Who are you, Edith? My eyes roved over the mostly happy, carefree faces.

And which one of these people killed you?

Chapter Five

I'D HEARD from Mrs. B that Barbara Hingley was a touch over eighty, but she certainly didn't look it. You'd never have guessed from her sprightly walk and sharp eyes that she was in her declining years. Her age really only showed in her wrinkled hands and thinning hair, the latter cropped close to her head.

She was also a giant pain in the rear end, if you want the unvarnished truth. Whether her daughter Kim was much better was debatable. I'd known this well before I saw them get out of their car at Baird House the following Saturday; I'd foolishly volunteered to take care of their hotel arrangements, hoping a little bonding might help me get some scraps of information about Edith.

I'd exchanged many more emails with both of them than the task should have required. Their list of demands would have put a movie star to shame. They had to have separate bedrooms, each with a king bed, none of that two queens business we hotel people were always trying to pull. Barbara snored, and Kim always left a light on. Neither would get a lick of sleep if I forced them to stay together, and what kind of invitation was that, if they weren't going to get a lick of sleep the whole time?

And speaking of invitations, they'd been waiting years for somebody to have the basic manners to invite them to Baird House and Tybryd, and they weren't about to be cheated out of a single bit of their splendor. They had to have mountain views, and if I could work in Tybryd's famous ferris wheel, so much the better.

They had to have a particular brand of bottled water in their in-room refrigerators—but not the same brand for each. The hotel didn't regularly carry either. And Kim had sent me a separate message instructing that there was to be *no vodka* in Barbara's fridge, or the consequences would be dire. I guessed the particulars of those consequences were above my pay grade, because I was given none.

In addition to their other travel requirements, Kim had informed me that they NEVER flew (just like that, in all caps), and declared her intention to drive her and her mother up from Georgia. I just bet that would be a fizzing time.

At least it was just the two of them. Both women were widows, despite Kim being, by my guess when I saw her in person, in the back half of her fifties. Maybe it was the tragedy of losing her husband that made her so mean. She had three kids, all of whom were out of the house now. That was all I knew; I didn't relish chatting with her so much that I asked for a lot of details.

I had, however, managed to work in a request for

Edith's picture. No such luck; they had none. Either she'd hated having her photograph taken and avoided it, or the family had destroyed what photos there were after they blackened her reputation. Barbara leaned toward the latter. Kim agreed. Both made it very clear at every opportunity that as far as they were concerned, the Tybryd Bairds had done Edith wrong—the skeleton proved that—and Mrs. B and her children owed Barbara and Kim a debt.

They did have quite a few photos of Edith's son (and Barbara's father) John, including one they'd scanned digitally. Kim forwarded that one to me, and promised to bring a few more. My first thought when I saw John's face was that, whatever rumors they'd spread about Edith later on, nobody could have accused her of sleeping around during her brief marriage. I had a couple of photographs of Roderick, and the resemblance between him and John was more than a little uncanny. The son was the spitting image of the father. He might have been Roderick's ghost, come back to haunt his family for mistreating his wife so.

Which gave me no clues whatsoever as to what Edith looked like, and was no help at all in identifying her in the midsummer party photograph.

Kim had left an hour later than planned, but failed to mention that until they were nearly due, which left those of us who were invited to their welcome lunch waiting quite a while. Not to mention those who'd actually done the work for the welcome lunch. Snick told me Dante was swearing up a storm in the kitchen.

But their car rolled up Baird House's long drive at

last, past the signature rhododendrons and up under the shadow of the famous red roof. Honestly, I couldn't blame them for craving an invitation. I'd been pretty excited myself, the first time I came here, and I still got a little thrill every time I drove that same path. I still looked up and said hello to the stone gargoyles and ravens under whose watchful eyes this house had prospered since the century before the last one.

Barbara and Kim seemed to feel no such whimsy, and no such thrill. It sounded like they were bickering when they got out of the car. They'd texted me when they were a minute or two out, and the other lunch guests had come outside to meet them. Besides Mrs. B, Percy, and me (and Plant), there was Basil Radcliffe, who owned Bryd Hollow's antique shop, his wife Erin, who'd been helping him out there since she'd retired from her job as a nurse last spring, and Lilian Berk, Tybryd's art director.

Mrs. B had followed Barbara's instruction to put out feelers for potential buyers, and both Basil and Lilian were anxious to meet Barbara and see the pieces—especially the watch—in person. So anxious, evidently, that they were willing to come outside in January to suck up to a cranky old woman, rather than just waiting in the dining room with a glass of wine. Either that, or they were just dead bored after sitting in that dining room for an extra hour already.

Snick was out there with us, of course, and started unloading the ladies' luggage from the trunk. His pale brows barely twitched when Kim told him, as if this somehow needed to be said, to be sure to use the handles on the suitcases. The man was just that good.

"Who are you, again?" Barbara asked me, as Mrs. B was introducing everybody.

I repeated my name, thinking Snick closing the trunk must have prevented her hearing it the first time. I assumed I didn't have to elaborate beyond that, considering how many times we'd talked over email, but Barbara looked blank.

"She's that dog waitress, Mother," said Kim. She looked a lot like Barbara, if you replaced the gray with obviously dyed brown hair that was two shades darker than I thought advisable with her pale, aging skin.

I heard a little bubble of surprised laughter escape Lilian Berk, while Percy quickly corrected Kim, declaring my official title to be Director of Canine Services. I voiced no objection, myself. I agreed that *dog waitress* was an odd descriptor, especially considering I had not once spoken to either Kim or Barbara in that capacity. But it wasn't entirely inaccurate, and I'd certainly been called worse.

Kim cast a suspicious glare at Plant. "And this is one of your customers?"

Apparently Barbara hadn't noticed Plant until then, because she screeched and jumped back with surprising agility for a person of any age, much less hers. "What is *that*?"

Plant started toward her; he often interpreted frightened cries as invitations to play. I grabbed his collar and told him to sit. "This is my dog, Plantagenet. I know he's a little big, but I promise he's—"

Barbara had already lost interest and turned to Kim.

"Give her Tabitha, then, if she's the pet server. Tabby can go to the hotel ahead of us and have a rest."

"We didn't stop at Tybryd to check in." Kim directed this comment to me, as if that were somehow my fault. As she spoke, she opened the back door of her car and leaned inside. "You all seemed so anxious for us to get here. Like that lunch was going to rot or something."

She emerged again with a cat carrier. "But she certainly can't stay here with that *dog*, so either she goes or he does."

"I don't suppose there's any way they could both go?" Erin Radcliffe asked. She gave Mrs. B a sheepish look. "I detest animals, if you want the truth."

"Oh!" Mrs. B pressed her hand to her chest. From the look of sympathy on her face, Erin might have just told her she had terminal cancer. "I had no *idea*."

That made two of us; this hadn't come up in the hour Plant had already spent sleeping in the corner of the dining room. If I'd known, I'd have left him home. But Percy and I had come together from my apartment, and I didn't have my own car to do anything about it now. I'd just have to put him—Plant, not Percy—in another room while we ate.

"Of course they can't *both* go!" Kim stared aghast at Erin. "Not unless it's in separate cars."

"Well, the cat definitely has to go!" Basil had stepped back almost to the front door, and was gaping at the cat carrier like it held a bomb. "I'm allergic to cats."

"Violently allergic," Erin added.

"That settles it, I suppose." Kim thrust the cat-or-maybe-a-bomb into my hands. A small gray tabby cat (tabby, Tabitha, how very clever) peered up at me from the other side of the carrier's wire door, tail swishing. "I assume your little daycare thing can handle a cat?"

"Um. Yessss." Even though Tailbryd was officially a dog daycare, we had put in a cat room, just in case. But I doubted we had any cat food on hand. People didn't tend to bring their cats on vacation, and on the rare occasion when they did, they tended to leave them in their rooms. Cats were more independent creatures, and just didn't need playgroups and grooming the way dogs did. "I didn't realize you'd be bringing a cat."

I tried not to sound critical about it, but honestly. How could you exchange that many emails—and demands—about travel arrangements and fail to mention a pet?

"I bring Tabitha everywhere." Barbara's affronted look clearly suggested this was common knowledge that I should have known without having to be told.

"I'm sure we can work it out," said Percy. Only those of us who knew him well would know his jovial smile was forced. "I'll just have to make sure you're in pet-friendly rooms."

"And do you have her vaccination records with you?" I asked.

Barbara waved that away. "I'm sure our vet can send you something. Kim will get it."

I looked at Percy. He was the one with the car, but I also knew he was starving. I didn't want him to lose any of his lunch to chauffeuring a cat around. "Ned's working. He probably wouldn't mind getting out of there for a bit to come and pick her up."

He smiled. "I'm sure he wouldn't. He's got a crush on you."

I rolled my eyes. "Ned is twenty-two. He does not have a crush on me. You think everybody's got a crush on me."

"Everybody with sense does." Percy pulled out his phone. "I'll check on those rooms while you talk to him."

As predicted, Ned was agreeable to coming to get Tabitha. Percy and I both offered to wait outside with her (it wasn't very cold, and Ned wouldn't be another ten minutes or so), but Snick practically begged for the job. Or actually, literally begged for it.

"Please," he muttered to me under his breath. "Please save me from waiting on these women."

I tried not to laugh as I handed him the cat carrier and thanked him for his service. In deference to Erin's sensibilities, I took Plant to the cavernous basement-level kitchen for one of the bones I kept there for emergencies, and told him to hang out with Dante (who was indeed fit to be tied, although Plant always cheered him up).

A shame Erin didn't also detest petite, nerdy ex-teachers; the kitchen smelled so good, I wouldn't have minded hiding in there with my dog and Dante for the rest of the afternoon. The mini pot pies sitting on the warming tray looked delectable, and I'd surely enjoy them more down here. But duty called—and I really wanted a look at the mysterious book with the bear cover.

"They're finally here," I said. "You can start serving whenever you want. Snick's outside babysitting their cat."

Dante let out a booming laugh. He was a giant man

with a long ponytail and several tattoos; you would never have imagined him capable of a delicate sauce or a platter of exquisite petits fours. "Working off some sins, I guess?"

"Actually, he preferred it to the alternative. Anything you want me to bring up?"

"Nah, the day maids don't mind serving."

"Yeah, but I'm going that way."

He entrusted a basket of biscuits to me, and sent me on my way. Not a moment too soon, as it turned out. When I walked into the dining room, Barbara was sitting at the head of the table, unwinding a hand towel from around the book like she was unwrapping a present. Basil and Lilian were already standing behind her, leaning in for a closer look.

I went over and squeezed myself sideways between Lilian and Percy, who was sitting to Barbara's left. He offered me the chair and when I refused, shifted it to give me more room. He put his hand on the small of my back, his thumb tracing little circles there.

But this was no time to be thinking about Percy Baird's hands, nice as they were. (And they really were very nice.) The small book—no bigger than a grocery-store paperback—was bound up tightly in clear plastic wrap, so it couldn't be opened to display the yellowed pages, but I could see they were thick and roughly cut, with uneven edges. The cover was soft brown leather. It looked like a journal or a sketchbook.

I assumed the design on the front was engraved or stamped in some way, but I didn't know much about leather working. The main thing was that it was a bear, inside a circle of leaves that, by their shape, looked like ash. Mrs. B had already set Edith's necklace, ring, and watch on the table, so I could see the medallion and the book side by side: there was no question it was the same bear.

It wasn't scientific, but it was good enough for me. I'd never seen that symbol before, and neither had anybody else I'd asked. Maybe it wasn't unique, but it wasn't common. I was comfortable stipulating that whoever owned that medallion also owned the book. There was no longer any question in my mind, probably because there hadn't been much to begin with, that the skeleton and Barbara's grandmother were one and the same.

"The pendant is interesting," said Basil. "It's almost like an old coin."

"Nobody used coins that big, did they?" Erin asked. She was sitting three seats away, but leaning forward on one outstretched elbow to peer at the necklace.

"Sure," said Lilian, "coins have come in all sorts of sizes through the centuries."

"And the design isn't something the Cotswolds ever used, that you know of?" I asked Barbara. "No bear in the family crest?" I'd already asked the same question of Mrs. B, who denied the presence of a bear in anything Baird-related she'd ever seen.

"That's not a family crest." Barbara glared at me. Maybe she found family crests offensive. "Probably just some picture Edith thought was pretty."

I started to ask what was inside the book, but was interrupted by Snick ushering Ned into the dining room.

Thankfully they didn't have Tabitha with them, so there was no Basil crisis to be managed. Ned assured Barbara that her cat was safe in his warm-but-not-hot car, and that he'd just popped in for her vaccination records.

"Can't check her in without those," he said.

Barbara scoffed. "I already told your friend, the vet has those. Obviously. It's not like I give her the shots myself." She flapped a hand at Kim. "Call Dr. Beverly and have him email something over."

Kim stood and jerked her head at Ned, who went to join her by the sideboard while she made the call. He was almost immediately obliged to move out of the way of two day maids, who came in with the pot pies and a giant bowl of caesar salad.

"I believe we're having caprese salad as well," Mrs. B said to Barbara, "and there's a different plate of pies, for the vegetarians."

Barbara completely ignored her, snapping her fingers instead at Ned. He blinked at her like she was some sort of alien creature. I supposed he wasn't used to being treated like one of the dogs.

"You can bring her to my room after dinnertime," she said. "You'll have to ask for the room number at the desk, I haven't checked in yet."

"Oh, we don't usually drop off—" I started, but Ned gave me a tiny wave.

"It's fine, I can bring her," he said. "But no later than five. I've got to get to the high school tonight."

"The high school?" Barbara looked mildly horrified. "You're not a *student*?"

I not-very-subtly covered a laugh behind my hand.

With his ginger hair and freckles and wide eyes, Ned did look pretty young. It didn't help that he blushed as he told Barbara he was not a student, not even a college one anymore.

Basil looked up from his examination of the watch and smiled at him. "Going to *Camelot*?"

"My cousin's playing Merlin," Ned said with a nod.

"Oh!" Erin said. "Basil's great-nephew is Sir Lionel!"

Both relayed their relatives' roles with a little more pride than they probably warranted. In a town the size of Bryd Hollow, even a high-school production was an event, especially in the winter when tourist events were few and far between. While they talked, I quickly took out my phone and snapped a couple pictures of the book; I already had some pictures of Edith's things, and wanted to complete the set. I hadn't asked permission, but I was sure Barbara wouldn't hesitate to let me know if she had any objections.

The door bumped Ned again, and the maids came in with more plates. He shuffled out of the way while Kim sent Tabitha's records from her phone to his. Mrs. B expressed her regrets that he couldn't stay for lunch, owing of course to the need to get Tabitha out of his car and into more comfortable accommodations (far away from Basil and Erin). Ned didn't look too broken up about it.

"Good luck," he whispered to me on his way out.

Everybody was hungry, lunch being so late, so it was agreed that the antiques should be stowed away until we finished eating. I wasn't about to let that stop me from asking about the book, though. I was more than a little eager to get a closer look at it, to see if it held any clues about Edith's murder.

"Is it Edith's journal, by chance?" I asked Barbara.

"Minerva's trying to put together what might have happened to Edith," said Percy. "It might help, if it's a journal."

"It's not a journal," Barbara snapped. "It's just a book of poetry."

"Can I read it?" I asked.

"Absolutely not! It's very old, and it's delicate. I never take off the plastic."

No? my inner voice asked. *Never?* Because that plastic had looked pretty fresh. She at least took it off to change it every so often.

By the look on her face, I was pushing my luck, but I bravely pressed on. "I'd wear gloves."

Basil jumped in to help me out, bless him. "I'll need to open it anyway, if I'm going to appraise it."

He earned a scowl from Barbara for his trouble. "You're not going to appraise it. It's not for sale. It has great sentimental value. It's the only thing of my grandmother's I have."

It *was* the only thing of her grandmother's she had, maybe. But now she had three more things, and those didn't have sentimental value? Was that because they were worth more? The watch certainly was, and maybe the necklace. Probably not the wedding ring, though. And wasn't a wedding ring a much more sentimental object than a book?

With what I considered a heroic effort, I refrained from asking any of these questions. She obviously wasn't in a very forthcoming mood, and they would only offend her more. I wanted to avoid sounding accusatory.

But I was definitely *feeling* accusatory. She was being weird about that book.

Barbara Hingley was hiding something.

Chapter Six

I'D BEEN ATTENDING church at St. Asaph's with the Bairds—Percy, Mrs. B, Elaine, and Elaine's husband Phil —every Sunday since summer. It was definitely a sign that I was considered family, or nearly so. The question was by whom—and how "nearly" we were talking.

The morning after Barbara and Kim arrived, Percy and I were supposed to pick them up at Tybryd to bring them with us. Everybody had left them to their own devices the night before (their idea, not ours, but don't think we weren't all relieved), so I hadn't seen Barbara since yesterday's lunch. I spent the ride to Tybryd in Percy's old Jeep chewing at my thumbnail and trying to think of ways I could interrogate her without appearing to interrogate her. The contents of a book that was probably a hundred and fifty years old and ostensibly of interest only to the family of its owner wasn't the sort of thing you could easily slide into small talk.

All thoughts of antiques and subtlety fled when we got close enough to the front entrance to see an ambulance parked at the curb. And two police cars parked behind it. Bryd Hollow didn't have so many police cars that seeing two in one place was a usual thing.

Percy and I exchanged worried looks as we hopped out of the Jeep and hurried inside. "What happened?" he asked the valet as we passed, without slowing his stride much.

The valet shrugged. "Nobody tells me anything."

Guests and staff alike were gathered in clumps in the lobby, murmuring amongst themselves. I didn't see the EMTs or the police, which must have meant they were in somebody's room.

Percy made a beeline for the front desk. "What happened?" he asked, for the second time in as many minutes.

The kid behind the desk—his name tag declared him to be Todd—couldn't have been twenty yet. He looked terrified, mainly of Percy. "I don't know for sure, but I think someone's *dead*. Hingley. Room 349."

I gasped. Percy blinked at him.

"You're sure that's the room?" I asked.

We barely waited for him to nod before running to the stairs. This was no time to wait on either Todd or an elevator.

The hallway outside room 349 was empty of the anxious crowd we'd seen in the lobby. Maybe the police had sent them all down there. The end closer to Kim's adjoining room 351 was occupied by Roark and another police officer, both talking to an apparently ranting Kim. She was turned so I could only see part of her profile, but that was enough to see that her face was red, and her mouth was moving a mile a minute. Unfortunately for me and Percy, it was a quiet rant. I couldn't make out a word.

Roark saw us and briefly raised his hand in a *be with you in a minute* sort of gesture. Kim didn't seem to notice.

Jo, the weekend concierge, leaned against the wall a few feet away from the closed door of Barbara's room, hands folded in front of her, like she was waiting in line. She looked scared and sick.

I decided to take over the *what happened* duties, and posed the question to her.

She replied much as Todd had, her voice barely above a whisper. "Mrs. Hingley is *dead*."

"But there's an ambulance outside," I said hopefully. Even though I got the distinct feeling from Jo's wan face that there was no hope. "Any chance she's not *quite* dead?"

"You must have missed the EMTs on your way up," said Jo. "And believe me, I'm sure. Mrs. Hollander was so upset, she didn't even call 911. She ran downstairs and started shrieking at *me* about what kind of place are we running here, where a woman can be robbed and killed in her own room. So I ran up here while I was calling 911, and—"

She shook her head, eyes tearing up. Percy squeezed her shoulder, but neither of us pressed her to go on before she was ready. (Even though I kind of wanted to.)

When she spoke again, her voice was thick. "I'm supposed to be giving these guys a statement when Mrs. Hollander is done. Because I was the second one who saw the b—" She cut herself off and swallowed. "I don't even know if I'm supposed to talk to you before I talk to them."

"I'm sure it's fine," Percy assured her. I assumed he was sure of no such thing.

But apparently that was good enough for Jo. "Someone hit her over the head with the desk lamp. You know, those ugly gold and pink ones Rex bought last year for some of the rooms, remember? I told him I didn't think those lamps were a good idea."

"I do remember," I said quietly. "Those lamps are heavy."

Jo nodded. "Mrs. Hingley was on the floor. Face down, thank goodness, so I didn't have to see her face. From the—" She gestured vaguely at the back of her head, then took a shuddering breath before going on. "It looked like maybe whoever did it hit her from behind. And there was a bunch of blood, and the lamp was on the floor. The bulb was broken. There were little pieces of it everywhere. Someone hit her hard enough to break the *bulb*."

She pressed her hand to her lips. "And that sweet little cat was curled up on the bed, just staring at me. Poor thing. Its eyes were so wide. I think Mrs. Hollander was allowed to put it in her room."

Percy jerked his head toward Barbara's door. "Who's in there now? Ruby?"

"I haven't seen Ruby. It's—"

Jo never got to finish her sentence, but it didn't really matter who was in there; we weren't going to get to talk to them. Apparently Kim had just noticed us—and she had some things to say.

She marched toward us, screaming at Percy the whole way. "What kind of place *is* this? My mother's things were *stolen*! From her own room! She was *murdered* in her own room! You call this a luxury resort? What's so *luxurious* about being *unsafe*? It must have been one of your people who did it! Unless your locks don't work! Do your locks not work?"

This went on for quite a while in much the same vein, peppered with threats to call the press and the "safety board," whoever that might mean. I might have understood and forgiven it, considering the woman had just lost her mother to a violent crime.

Except I hadn't missed her choice of words: *stolen* had distinctly come before *murdered*. Like that was the more salient point. People responded to death in all kinds of ways that were beyond judging. Even so, I found her priorities a bit odd.

As for what was stolen, it seemed like it would be some time before we could get a word in to ask. But I had a feeling I already knew.

THAT NIGHT, Percy and I curled up on my couch with Plant and two very generous cocktails, and rented a movie. Which probably sounds heartless, but we hadn't known Barbara so well that we were personally grieving, and it had been a long day—especially for Percy. In addition to all the other hardships presented by a death both in the family and in one's place of business, two news sites had already contacted him for comment. Kim was going to make sure there was a scandal, if she possibly could. And she probably could.

And as he'd already said earlier in the day, the worst part of that was that she might be right to. Or rightish, anyway. I'd always heard that most people were murdered by somebody they knew, but the only person in Bryd Hollow who knew Barbara was her daughter. So either Kim had done it, or a stranger had gotten into Barbara's room. Maybe the killer was a hotel employee, or somebody posing as one, or maybe they'd physically broken in. None of those possibilities exactly reflected well on Tybryd.

To the surprise of nobody, Kim had declared her mortal fear of staying at Tybryd another night, which put Mrs. B in a tough position. She felt obligated to invite Kim and Tabitha to stay at Baird House while the police sorted out what happened. Kim and Barbara had, after all, come to Bryd Hollow as Mrs. B's guests, and they were family besides. Mrs. B seemed to feel tremendously guilty. I understood the sentiment; I probably should have had more compassion for Kim myself, and would have, had she not gone after Percy so hard.

The downside of course was that such an arrangement would put Percy directly in Kim's line of fire on a daily basis. In the end, Mrs. B had extended the invitation anyway, and Percy had resolved to stay at the office or my apartment as much as possible.

The movie was bad, but that was probably a good thing; I wasn't really watching, and I'd have hated to miss something good. I couldn't focus on anything except Barbara's murder.

There were no obvious suspects, in the sense of the police finding somebody roaming the halls with blood splattered on their shirt. No witnesses. Kim said she hadn't heard anything the night before. This morning she'd gone through the adjoining door to her mother's room to ask if she was ready for church, and found her dead on the floor still wearing last night's clothes.

As I'd surmised, Roderick Baird's watch was gone, as were Edith's ring and necklace. Even the book was gone. Barbara's wallet was still intact, credit cards and all. Her in-room safe had been open, but that didn't necessarily mean anything. The watch might not even have been in there; most people didn't keep things locked up when they were actually in their room.

Thanks to Tybryd's computer system, we could trace Barbara and Kim's movements the night before (for the police, of course, and not at all to poke our own noses into their investigation). Tabitha had been checked out of Tailbryd at the promised time, and a quick call to Ned confirmed that he'd dropped her off as planned. A charge to Kim's room indicated that she and her mother had dinner at one of Tybryd's restaurants a short while later. The server remembered them both (not terribly fondly). According to Kim, she then spent the night alone in her room watching a movie, as her mother was in the habit of going to bed right after dinner, being eighty-one and all. The system confirmed the movie rental, too.

But as I was at that very moment demonstrating, renting a movie, or even playing a movie, wasn't the same thing as watching a movie. I pressed the pause button on the remote—for the third time in the past hour—and sat up straight, displacing a very annoyed Plant's head from my lap. "You really think it was Kim?"

Percy didn't look annoyed by the interruption. I doubted he'd been paying any more attention than I had. He leaned forward and set his drink down on the coffee table. "I can't say I *definitely* think it was her. But if I were the police, she'd be my top suspect. She's acting weird."

"You mean not calling the police?" He'd mentioned that a few times already today, and I had to agree with him there. People did all sorts of things that didn't make sense when they were panicked. But going straight to the concierge to complain? Whose reflexive reaction was that?

But I supposed if it were anybody's, it would be Kim Hollander's. Or Barbara's, had their positions been reversed.

"It's not just that." Percy drummed his fingers against the side of his glass. "She's going out of her way to lay blame."

On him, no less. I gave him a sympathetic look. "People tend to do that when they're grieving."

"I know, but it feels like she's going a little over the top with it."

"You think it's an act to keep people from suspecting her." It wasn't a question; I already knew he thought that —or wanted to think it. It just didn't sit quite right with me. I chewed at my lip. "But why would Kim steal Edith's things?"

Percy spread his hands. "Same reason anybody else would. To sell them. You and I both know the watch was the only thing worth any serious money, but somebody else might not know that."

"Kim would, though. She was at lunch with Basil and Lilian, same as we were. And even if she did want to sell everything, if she was willing to kill her mother, she could've just stopped there. Then the things would've been hers."

"So maybe she just made it look like a robbery to throw suspicion off herself."

I shook my head. It still didn't feel right. "I can't find the connection to Edith."

His lips twitched. "That's probably because we weren't talking about Edith."

"But we should be."

"You're just saying that because you like her murder better."

I pursed my lips at him. "I'm saying that because they're connected. Look at the facts: Edith's grand-daughter is murdered at Tybryd—the same place Edith was—on the day she comes to help identify Edith's remains, and then only Edith's things are taken?"

"The theft isn't such a big coincidence. The watch is worth money, plain and simple. And the other things might not be worth as much, but even if the killer knew that, they're still antiques. They're worth something. Barbara probably came in and caught some guy, and he whacked her on the head and ran. Unless it was Kim"— Percy pointed at me for emphasis—"which it probably was."

"But if it wasn't, if it was your Some Guy, how did he get in her room? How did he know about the watch and stuff in the first place?"

These were also questions we'd already asked several times. The answers were, in order, *We don't know* and *Because this is Bryd Hollow*. It was a small town, and by now the mystery skeleton was as famous as any other Baird. Mrs. B, Basil, Lilian, Roark, Ruby, even the tree guy: anybody could have been talking to their friends about it. There were probably dozens of people who knew about the watch, pendant, and ring.

"But what about the book?" I said. "Only the people at lunch yesterday knew about that. Or at least, we were the only ones who actually saw it."

"He probably didn't know about the book," Percy said with a shrug. "It was probably just sitting with the other stuff, and he could see it looked really old, and figured he'd swipe that too."

This explanation, while the simplest and most obvious, was not my preferred one. "No. There is something weird about that book. Barbara was being weird about it."

He squeezed my knee. "I agree Barbara was weird about it, but that doesn't mean the book itself was weird. She seemed like a pretty weird lady overall."

"She was hiding something."

"Like what?" He leaned over to kiss my cheek. Like he thought I was being cute, and was laughing at me on the inside, which kind of made me want to punch him. Except I laughed at him all the time, too. "What grand conspiracy are you imagining, involving a book, that led to the murders of two women over a century apart?"

"I have no idea whatsoever," I admitted. "But we're going to find out."

"We?"

"Yes. You were patronizing just now—"

"I was not! When?"

"Just now. Yes you were. So now you have to help me."

"I don't quite follow the logic."

"So you can be there to see that I'm right and you're wrong, and apologize and buy me a nice dinner."

"We couldn't just skip to the dinner?"

"Nope."

He heaved an affected sigh, sounding so put upon that Plant raised his head to see what the problem was. "Fine. Where do we start?"

"Um ..." I had no idea whatsoever on that score, either. I raised my now empty glass. "How about with more bourbon?"

Chapter Seven

WHEN I'D STARTED RESEARCHING Edith Baird, I'd asked everybody I could think of in Bryd Hollow who might know what a bear in a circle of ash leaves meant: Basil, Lilian, the local librarian, a few of the high-school teachers. (Never underestimate the depth of a high-school teacher's knowledge.) I'd come up blank, and let it go in favor of other, higher priorities, like finding a photograph of Edith.

Now that bear seemed a little more important than it had before. It was time to revisit the topic. I went online and searched for every possible combination of a bear and a circle of ash leaves I could come up with. I checked on the existence of the surnames *Ashbear*, *Bearleaves*, *Leafybear*, and *Bearash* (I definitely would have changed that one, if it were real and my last name). I looked for places named *Ash Bear Circle*, *Ashburg*, *Bearton*, and *Leaf Bear Hill*.

I went on like that for the entirety of Monday evening. Sometimes I found place names that might have fit; there was Asheville, obviously, which wasn't far from us. But I didn't find anything that suggested even the remotest relationship to Edith Cotswold Baird.

It was Tuesday afternoon by the time I realized what an idiot I was. I was standing behind the desk at work, entering a dog's information into the database, when it hit me.

"There's such a thing as an image search, you know!"

Thankfully, said dog had already been shown to his kennel, and his owner had left. Only Taren was there. She blinked at me like maybe I was a crazy person.

"I have *pictures*!" I said.

"Of ... Loki? Are we supposed to put pictures in their files?"

My mouth dropped open, my own oversight temporarily forgotten in the face of hers. "Yes, you're supposed to put pictures in their files! You take one when you check them in, if they haven't been here before."

"Why?" Taren asked.

"What happens if Loki's owner comes to get him, and neither you or I are here? It's just Ned and say, Fiona, and Ned tells Fiona to grab Loki from kennel five, but she thinks he said nine? And neither of them knows what Loki looks like?"

"But Loki's owner knows what he looks like. He's not going to take the wrong dog."

"No, but we should also avoid trying to give him the wrong dog. It makes us look badly organized, and not very smart."

Frankly, both descriptions fit me more than I would've liked at the moment. I looked to rectify that as soon as Plant and I got home that night. We were on our own for dinner; Percy was working long hours dealing with the PR nightmare (and tragedy, of course) that was Barbara Hingley's murder. I put some kibble in Plant's bowl—then a little sprinkle of cheese, after the dirty look I got for the plain kibble—and settled for a bowl of cereal for myself. I didn't want to waste any more time than I already had.

I was confident this was the answer to everything. If I did a reverse image search on my pictures of the book and the medallion, surely the internet would spit back something along the lines of:

The bear-and-ash-leaf symbol was the exclusive personal symbol of Edith Cotswold Baird, who was murdered by John Smith at Tybryd, the same place her granddaughter Barbara Hingley was also murdered by Jack Doe. You can pick up proof of these crimes—along with a detailed and completely credible explanation as to how they're connected, which they definitely are—in the following locations, after which Percy will admit he was wrong and take you to a nice dinner.

This did not happen. The internet was just as befuddled by the bear as I was. Which did help me feel a little less stupid for not having asked it sooner, but didn't bring me any closer to identifying Edith's—or Barbara's —killer.

But if I didn't find a bear, I did find something similar enough to make my typing and scrolling fingers tingle with that sensation of being on to something. After a zoomed-in image of the design on the medallion didn't turn anything up, I fed the search a zoomed-out one, of the whole necklace.

It found a few matches for that. None of them exact, but all of them flat circles of silver with irregular edges bordered by a ring of leaves. The shape of the leaves varied, as did what was inside them: a bird, a tree, a Celtic cross, a candle, a goblet.

And because the internet knew where I lived, it kindly offered me the most local selection of these it could find, for my shopping convenience. The bird and the goblet were both for sale at the same antiques store: Holly Tree Lane of Poplar Knot, North Carolina.

At least, I thought it was an antiques store. Holly Tree Lane wasn't exactly a well branded name for a store, and its website wasn't much better. First of all, its color scheme, if it could be called that, appeared to be lime green, cyan, and flamingo pink, which were not very antique-y looking colors. They'd probably have had better luck selling glasses frames to Ruby Walker. It was a single page, with images of a mere seven items for sale. I assumed that was only a sampling, but who knew. Two were the bird and goblet medallions, with no chains attached. The other five were books, all clearly very old.

Four of the books bore no resemblance to Edith's, but one, leather bound like hers, had a circle of leaves (they looked more like pine needles) on the cover, with the same bird as the medallion in the middle. A raven or a crow, I thought, now that I could zoom in better. They must have been selling them as a matched set.

"But a matched set of *what*?" I asked Plant. "What

are these?" He was very tired, and offered no opinion on the matter.

The website wasn't very forthcoming, either. It didn't even have a phone number on it. What kind of business didn't have a phone? It did have an email address, but apart from that the only text was a subtitle below the name of the store (*a family business since 1938*), their business hours, and a declaration that they were pet friendly. I liked that part. But the hours were weird: they were only open Tuesday and Saturday, otherwise by appointment only.

"What is it, a part-time job for you people?" I was mostly asking myself; I'd given up on Plant.

Maybe that was exactly what it was. By the site, it wouldn't surprise me to learn it was an amateur operation. Maybe the younger generation was just keeping the family business nominally running for the sake of a grandparent or something.

A map search told me that the town of Poplar Knot was in the mountains, like Bryd Hollow, but further north, almost at the Virginia border. Taking mountain roads into account (and the fact that they made Percy carsick, which meant stopping occasionally) it would take us more than two hours to get there, probably closer to three.

I supposed the fastest and most direct course of action would be to send the Holly Tree people an email, attach the pictures of Edith's necklace and book, and ask what they were, what they had to do with the items on their website, and most importantly, what they had to do with the bludgeoning of both a woman and her grand-daughter, many years apart but at the same location.

My issues with that approach were threefold. First, it might be hard to compose an email like that without sounding a little bit like a nut.

Second, visiting Poplar Knot instead, and bringing Percy with me, would mean getting him out of town and away from Baird House. Kim was still staying there. At least she'd stopped being overtly confrontational, after Mrs. B had explained that the Baird family lawyer advised cutting off contact in case of any litigation. Kim had insisted, with much gasping and puffing, that she intended *no* such thing, it hadn't even crossed her *mind*, this was a *family* matter, and just because she'd been understandably and naturally upset didn't mean she wanted to *sue* anybody.

Percy took her enthusiastic interest in avoiding a courtroom as further evidence of her guilt. Personally, I considered it better evidence that she thought she could bully more out of Mrs. B than she could a judge. And do it with no lawyer's fees attached, besides. She'd already hinted several times that the Bairds ought to pay for her mother's funeral and other "final expenses," whatever those might be. And according to Roark, her harangues at the police were loudest when she was inquiring about the theft of the watch, rather than the murder of her mother. That she had more than a passing interest in money was hardly a secret.

Either way, her shift to passive-aggressively accusing Percy of as good as swinging the lamp himself wasn't a whole lot more pleasant than her doing it aggressive-aggressively. Heaven knew the man could use a break.

As for my third reason for wanting to go to Holly Tree Lane in person: I really wanted to see this place for myself.

~

As I'd expected, Percy was fully in favor of a short escape from Bryd Hollow and his life in general. We drove north on Friday night, Plant in the back of the Jeep, but stopped short of Poplar Knot, as they appeared to have no hotels within a many-mile radius. We found a pet-friendly place in Boone instead; we'd be able to have a leisurely breakfast in the morning and drive the further half hour to Poplar Knot in plenty of time for their ten o'clock opening.

We did just that—even Plant got his own pancake—and arrived in Poplar Knot early, which turned out to be a good thing, because the GPS didn't seem to understand Poplar Knot very well. It sent us the wrong way twice. Odd, considering it was a tiny town.

But it didn't have a main street the way normal towns did. It didn't even have a traffic light. It was a chaotic knot of maybe a dozen small roads winding around each other and grudgingly intersecting, when they absolutely had to, at four-way stops. The streets were lined with old Victorian houses, and no obvious stores or commercial buildings at all.

I supposed people here worked in Boone, which was no metropolis itself, but had a university. Or across the state line, where there was at least one other college that I knew of. But where did they go for groceries? Or take-out? Or medical attention? I was all for small towns, but a thirty-plus-minute drive away from food was small beyond my limits.

We knew they had at least one store, though not for necessities. But it wasn't easy to find. Holly Tree Lane was not, as its name might have suggested, on Holly Tree Lane, but on Poplar Avenue. As distinguished (but not very well) from Poplar Street, Poplar Lane, and Poplar Circle.

Plant was pretty cranky by the time we finally found it, and Percy and I weren't far behind. It was much like the other houses in Poplar Knot: big and rambling, with the signature Victorian turret on one side. It was painted a sunny, but not at all garish, yellow, which was more subtlety than I expected, after viewing their website. Neat rows of holly bushes lined the driveway and the front porch.

Its main difference from its neighbors was that it was on a much bigger lot, with a low, square building to the right of the house that might once have been a barn or a stable. A swinging sign on a post informed us that this building was, at last, Holly Tree Lane.

A bell above the door tinkled as we walked in, but assuming its purpose was to announce our presence, it was hardly necessary. The immediate yapping of a miniature pinscher must have done a fine job of that on its own. Neither his tail nor his ears had been cropped, which made me kindly disposed toward his owner. He trotted up to us—still barking—and raced in circles around Plant. Plant was all for this, and would have responded in kind had I not pulled his leash up closer to my side. An antiques shop (if that was what this was) was no place for a big dog to be lumbering around.

Apart from the minpin, the first thing I noticed about Holly Tree Lane was that it smelled divine, with some herbal mix I couldn't identify floating up from the multitude of candles burning inside the otherwise empty fireplace to our right. Two plush chairs sat in front of it, one with a little dog bed on it. To our left was another cozy seating area, this one with four chairs and a table between them. The wall on that side was lined with bookshelves taller than Percy. I didn't see any titles on the spines. The shop must have been only a small part of whatever they did here; this room was much smaller than the building.

A pair of twins emerged from a door behind the long wooden counter. Identical twins, technically, but nobody would ever have trouble telling these two apart. One looked like she'd answered a casting call for a stereotypical librarian: auburn hair in a tight bun, small round glasses, no makeup. The other had short hair dyed bright pink, and more neon eyeshadow than two eyelids ought to have been able to hold. I guessed I knew which one had designed the website. They looked young, college age or just past it.

"You brought a *dog*!" Pink Hair said with a happy squeal.

"Is he okay off leash?" Librarian asked. Her stare was intense. It was a little disconcerting, to be honest. "You should let them out, if he is. Just for a minute? Gravy wants to play, and yours doesn't look like he'd mind."

Plant was pretty good with small dogs, and he really did look like he wanted to play with this one, so I opened the door. Gravy zoomed out, while I unclipped Plant's leash and said, "Go ahead, go play."

The two dogs immediately started running laps around the yard. Not exactly chasing each other. Mostly just showing each other how fast they were. The twins followed us outside, both of them laughing.

"How can we help you?" Pink Hair asked.

I pulled out my phone. "I noticed some things on your website that looked like these. I was hoping you could tell me more about them." I moved between the young women, so they could both look at the pictures, and swiped between the medallion and the book.

With them both looking over my shoulders, I couldn't see their faces, but I could tell from Percy's that something was up.

"Um," Librarian began, but then nothing followed.

"You know what?" said Pink Hair. "If you could give us just one minute."

Librarian elbowed her. "You want us to leave them alone? I'll stay behind."

"No way, I need you as a witness," said Pink Hair. "She'll never believe me. Besides, Gravy will watch them."

Gravy was paying no attention to us whatsoever, but since I had no intention of robbing them, I didn't point this out.

"Excuse us," said Librarian, "Just one—"

"—sec," her sister finished, and then both were off, hurrying toward the house.

"What was that about?" I asked Percy.

"I don't know. They looked surprised. And I think the one with the"—he gestured at his head—"hair might have been a little scared."

Scared? I didn't know what to make of that, but I didn't doubt him. Percy was pretty good at reading people. I liked to think I was, too, but I didn't even have a wild guess as to what was going on here.

I didn't have to wait long to find out. It couldn't have been two minutes later—the dogs hadn't even gotten tired yet—when I heard a door slam in the distance, and the twins came back with a redhead in tow. I don't mean a strawberry blonde, or an auburn-head like the librarian, or an almost-chestnut-but-really-it's-brown-head like me. I mean a blazing, brilliant redhead, and her face had all the spirit to match. She looked older than the twins, but younger than my almost-thirty.

I immediately found her annoying. Mainly because she gave Percy a look that was more openly appreciative than I would have liked.

Then I reminded myself that it didn't matter that she was basically stunning, or that last December some magazine had named Percy one of America's one hundred most eligible bachelors, a thing that had definitely not freaked me out. Because I was a strong, confident woman who was above petty insecurities and jealousies.

Mostly. Usually.

All of that must have shown on my face, because when her eyes shifted to me she gave me a little smile that clearly said *Oh, I see. And good for you.* Maybe she wasn't so annoying.

Percy extended his hand and introduced himself. I supposed we should have done that already, with the twins. Then maybe I'd have real names for them instead of Librarian and Pink Hair.

"Autumn Trelayne," the new arrival said as she shook. She turned and whistled for Gravy, who immediately trotted over to her. Plant followed, tongue lolling. No matter what Autumn could or couldn't tell us, this trip wouldn't have been wasted; Plant was having a fizzing time.

"Autumn," Percy said in his Charming Small Talk voice (which to be one hundred percent honest, for a guy of his social status, could've been better). "Is that because of the red hair, or were you born in the fall?"

"I was born on Halloween, actually, so it could've been a lot worse." Autumn waved a hand at the twins, who were still just standing there, gawking at us. They'd clearly transferred all authority over this affair to her. "My cousins, Holly and Ivy. So you can see the theme. All Trelaynes get seasonal names."

At least Holly Tree Lane made sense now, if nothing else did. I supposed this Holly was named after whatever Holly Trelayne had founded the family business.

"Even dogs?" I asked, kneeling down to scratch Gravy's back. He climbed up onto my legs and put his front paws on my shoulders, to give me better access.

"Of course," Autumn said. "I said all family, didn't I?"

My opinion of her got another upgrade. "And Gravy was born in ...?"

"November. Just a few days before Thanksgiving. Shall we go inside?"

Percy and I followed her back into the shop, the twins behind us. Autumn led us to the four-chair seating area and gestured for us to sit, while Gravy hopped up on what was clearly his chair in front of the fireplace. Plant promptly jumped onto the chair beside the minpin, making himself right at home.

I started to tell him to get off—big dogs weren't always allowed on furniture, even when little dogs were —but Autumn stopped me.

"He's fine," she said. "Gravy loves to meet a good dog, and I can tell he—what's his name?"

"Plantagenet. Plant for short."

"I can tell Plant is a good dog. Aren't you, Plant?"

He thumped his tail. She nodded in return, as if he'd answered her in English. "Now." She sat down opposite me and folded her hands, elbows on the arms of the chair, expression all business. "Holly and Ivy tell me you've got a Mistmantle spellbook and focus, but I'll admit I'm skeptical. Can I see the pictures?"

I handed her my phone, wondering if I'd just misheard her. "I'm sorry, did you just say *spell*book?"

"Maybe she meant *spelling* book," Percy suggested. "Like a textbook."

"Ivy." Autumn sighed at Librarian, so I guessed now I knew which sister was which. Both twins were still standing near the door. "You might have said."

"I thought I did!" she protested.

"You didn't." Autumn glanced down at my phone. Then looked at it in earnest. The irritation in her face fled as she swiped from one picture to the other and back again. "Where did you get these?"

"We'll be happy to tell you, if you tell us what"— Percy flicked his hand between Autumn and Ivy—"that little exchange meant."

Autumn shot another annoyed look at her cousin as she handed my phone back to me. "I just assumed, with you coming in here asking about a focus and a spellbook, that at least one of you would be one of us. Ivy can tell, she's always had a knack for it, but I can't."

"One of us? As in ... a Trelayne?" Percy looked confused. "We don't even have seasonal names."

I was less confused. She'd just used the word *spellbook* a second time, and I couldn't have misheard her twice. I had a feeling I knew what was coming.

"No," said Autumn. "As in *witches*."

Chapter Eight

HIGHLIGHT/LOWLIGHT of our visit to Holly Tree Lane: The lowlight was obviously the whole witchcraft thing. I didn't like to think that my only real lead was coming from a crackpot.

But Autumn turned out to be a likable crackpot, and the biggest highlight—apart from Plant making a fine new friend—was the way she put Percy in his place. Much as I loved him, I admitted this was occasionally necessary, and usually entertaining to watch. Percy was never rude or unkind—never on purpose, anyway—but his firm conviction that he was funny could get him into trouble sometimes. And because most people treated him like a golden boy and indulged him, he was rarely aware of said trouble.

Upon hearing the word *witches*, he gave Autumn a grave nod. "I can see how you wouldn't realize we are too, given how we arrived. It's just the dog isn't great on a broom."

"Well, no, he wouldn't be," Autumn said, matching

her deadpan tone to his. "Obviously we attach sidecars for dogs."

She waited for Percy's chuckle, then nodded back at him. "The sidecar thing was a joke. The witch thing wasn't."

"I ... oh." He blinked at her. "I'm sorry, I—"

"No, it's fine. Please do go on as if I were joking. Best for all of us, really. We don't usually discuss it with strangers."

"She doesn't mean stranger-strangers." Holly stepped closer to us, apparently no longer content to stay out of the conversation. Maybe because Autumn had taken my pictures seriously, and was still calm about it. Percy had said Holly looked a little scared before, but now her eyes were bright with excitement. "We don't talk about it much with people we know, either, if they're strangers."

"*Strangers* is our word for non-magical folk," Ivy supplied. She was still hanging back a little more, but her face was just as eager as her sister's. "And it's not that we don't talk about it at *all*. It's fine if they already know. But we don't announce it if they don't."

"Thank you both." Autumn inclined her head toward the door behind the counter. "How about you guys go back to what you were doing? Or find something new to do, as long as it's not in here."

"But we want to know about the book!" Holly protested.

"And the focus!" Ivy added.

"And I'll fill you in. But five is too many in a conversation. Three is better. And there aren't enough chairs for all of us anyway." Autumn flapped her hand at them. "Go."

I didn't call attention to the obvious fact that there would have been enough chairs for all of us, if each dog didn't have his own. The twins looked a little mutinous, but they went into the back room whence they'd come when we first walked in, and closed the door behind them.

"Okay, so if you weren't joking, maybe you could throw a fireball or something," said Percy. "You know, just so we know what we're dealing with here."

"Careful," I said, "she might throw it at you."

Autumn spread her hands. "Sorry, no parlor tricks. Magic requires *spells*. It's not immediate. We're not Carrie at the prom." She quirked a smile at me. "Besides, he's too cute to light on fire."

"Sometimes," I agreed.

"Oh come on," said Percy. "I am always too cute to *light on fire*. That's a pretty low bar."

"And we don't mind a bit if strangers think we're kooks," Autumn went on. "We greatly prefer laughter to the alternative."

"Because if people took it seriously they might ask for favors?" Percy leaned forward in his chair, clearly struggling to keep a straight face. "Like ask you to turn straw into gold?"

Autumn gave him a mild look. "More because there's kind of a long history of not-witches doing mean things to witches. You should look it up."

I didn't bother trying to stifle my laugh at Percy's expense. My decision was made: I officially liked Autumn

Trelayne. "So, speaking of spellbooks," I said, "I gather this Mistmantle spellbook belonged to somebody named Mistmantle?"

"A lot of somebodies," said Autumn. "Spellbooks are family affairs, handed down through the generations. Except the Mistmantle family died out in the last century, which brings me back to my question of where you got it."

"Are we sure it's a spellbook?" Percy asked. I could practically hear the finger quotes around *spellbook* in his voice, but at least he refrained from actually making them. "It might just be an old journal or something, no? None of us has seen the inside of it."

Autumn's brow furrowed. "You didn't look inside?"

"Long story," I said. "Somebody was being weird, which is what got me investigating it in the first place. Do spells rhyme?"

She waggled her hand. "Sometimes. Especially older ones."

Percy flashed the dimples. "Double double toil and trouble, and so forth?"

"She told us it was a book of poetry," I said to Percy. "Remember?"

"Well, obviously I can't say for sure that it's a spell-book without seeing it," said Autumn. "But if I can authenticate the items, and you came by them by legitimate means, I'd love to buy them from you."

"We don't actually have them," I said.

"They belonged to my cousin." Percy glanced at me. "Cousin? Something cousin something removed, right?" He waved a hand before I could work out Barbara's exact relationship to him, assuming he meant Barbara and not Edith. "Doesn't matter. They belonged to a relative. Not named Mistmantle."

I noted he left a lot out of that story, presumably because he didn't trust the kooky witch. I played along, and didn't elaborate on the whole murder thing. Instead I added, "Actually, there are no Mistmantles in the Baird family tree. I've dabbled in their genealogy a little bit, and I've never heard the name before."

"So where are the focus and the book now?" Autumn asked. I didn't know her well (or at all), but I was pretty sure that was impatience creeping into her voice.

I didn't mention that we had no idea, for fear she'd give up on us. I still needed information. "By 'the focus,' I gather you mean the pendant?"

"Yes. It's exactly what it sounds like: witches sometimes use them to focus their magic." Her hand drifted up to her throat, fingers fidgeting with the collar of her turtleneck, and I wondered whether she had a pendant of her own under there. "They don't make them as much anymore, but I still come by a powerful antique now and then. They're very valuable to my folk."

"So this is what you do?" I looked around the shop: the bookshelves lined with old books, the scented candles, the two snoring dogs. I didn't see any other medallions, but I knew from their website that they had at least two. "You sell old spellbooks and ... magic stuff?"

Autumn gestured broadly in the direction of the books. "Spellbooks and spells, mostly. Ivy and some of the other family write new spells. I'm the one who digs up the old ones, from estate sales and such. Or sometimes families just don't want their spellbooks anymore. Either they're not practicing, or they've gone digital and would rather have the money than the paper copy."

She turned to Percy. "Look. You clearly don't know any witches. The book and the focus won't be worth anything to you or your something cousin something removed. But I could sell them both for quite a bit. I'm sure we could come up with a fair arrangement."

"They're not mine to sell." He scratched the back of his neck. "That, and they were both stolen."

She flattened her lips, her eyes taking on a determined look that suggested she might go out and look for them right that minute. "Any leads?"

"Not yet," said Percy.

"That's why we came here, actually," I said. "They were taken along with something else that was more valuable, an antique watch, that the police think was probably the real object of the theft—"

"That's because it was the real object of the theft," Percy interjected.

"Be that as it may," I said, tossing him a weary look. "It's good to have all the information we can, right? They did take the book and the pendant, and I noticed you had similar things on your website, so I hoped you could tell us more about them. You all seemed to recognize them right away, I guess because of the bear and the ash leaves?"

"Rowan leaves," said Autumn. "And yes, we're definitely familiar with the Mistmantles' emblem, dealing in old things as we do. The Mistmantles are sort of a legend among my folk. They were very powerful, and not in a good way."

"Black magic?" Percy whispered, his eyes fake-wide. Thankfully, my chair was close enough to his for me to smack his knee.

Autumn leaned into conspiring distance and dropped her voice in turn. "Turning people into newts. And *worse*."

She straightened back up. "But the last of the Mistmantles died in World War I."

"Fighting for the US?" I asked. "Were they American?"

"They were." Autumn rested her right elbow on the arm of her chair and tapped each of her fingers against her thumb, going back and forth in order. "I know they lived in Baltimore, because I always thought that was funny, considering their life was kind of like a Poe story. Lester was his name. Or actually I couldn't swear to that, it could've been Leonard. But I remember it was just him and his sister Matilda left when their parents died. The tragic siblings, last of a great and terrible house, all that stuff."

Matilda. Why was that name striking me as significant? *Lester.*

"Then she died," Autumn went on. "I think of some old-timey disease, consumption or something, and it was just him. So the family died with him, and their book was never found. It was presumed rotted in a trench somewhere."

I shook my head. "He didn't have it when he died.

The pendant was found on the body of a woman who died in 1913."

Autumn's eyes shot wide. "What woman?"

"Her name was Edith Baird. And we've been told the book was passed down from her too, so unless that's not true, she had the book a year before the war broke out, and four years before the US joined it."

"So how did Edith get the book from Lester-or-Leonard?" Percy cocked his head at me. "I thought the Cotswolds were English."

"They were," I said absently. I was still thinking about the names Matilda and Lester. They sounded so familiar. Not that they were uncommon to that period, but still. Something about them together was tugging at me. Had I come across these Mistmantles somewhere before, after all?

"The Mistmantle family was originally British, I think," said Autumn. "In which case, they probably made trips over there now and then. It's not uncommon for the old families to get in touch with their magical roots, if they have the means. Sometimes the literal roots. There will be spots that are powerful for them. Maybe this Edith met Lester-or-Leonard there."

I was vaguely aware that what she was saying would have been interesting to me, had I been listening better— but I'd just remembered.

I pulled my phone back out, not for the photos this time, but for the browser. "When exactly did Matilda die?" I asked as my thumbs moved over the screen. "And how sure are you about the cause of death?"

"I don't know exactly," said Autumn, "but definitely

81

a few years before her brother. And anyway he was older, so he'd most likely have had the book."

"He didn't." I glanced up. "And you were right the first time. His name was Lester."

"You just found him?" Percy asked.

"Not him." I set my phone on the table between us, angled so they could both see it. I'd pulled up the *Titanic* passenger list I'd first found Edith and Roderick Baird on. As was often the case with the wealthy, they weren't the only ones in their party. I pointed at the name below Edith's, while Autumn and Percy leaned in closer.

The entry had a cross next to it, indicating the passenger in question had perished that night.

Lester, Miss Tilly (Maid to Mrs. Roderick Robert Baird), 21, †

Chapter Nine

"So EDITH's lady's maid was a witch." Percy merged onto the road that would take us away from the almost literal knot that was Poplar Knot. Plant was passed out in the back seat, exhausted from his ten minutes of play followed by a half hour of napping. "A witch who was traveling under a false name, as a servant, for reasons we don't know and maybe never will."

Even he didn't doubt that much, skeptical as he was about the rest. The combination of Matilda's name and her brother's, combined with the fact that her employer had ended up with the Mistmantles' things, was too big a coincidence to ignore.

"And Edith must have believed in witchcraft," I said, "or she wouldn't have taken the necklace and the book. I mean how many things could you bring with you on a lifeboat off the *Titanic*, and that's what she picks? Maybe your mother had it wrong. Maybe she wasn't a *witch with a B*. Maybe she was just a *witch with a W*."

Percy chuckled. "Or maybe she just knew there were

a bunch of crazy people who thought they were witches around, who would pay a lot for that kind of thing. It didn't sound like Roderick was a hundred percent confident that his family would take care of her and the baby. Maybe she needed a backup plan."

I wasn't sure how I felt about any of those possibilities. I'd felt protective of Edith from the moment Mrs. B had told us her story. Or maybe even before that; maybe from the moment they'd found her bones at my dog daycare. But the idea that she'd stolen her maid's valuables before hopping on a lifeboat and leaving the rest of her party to die made her look the tiniest bit like a ratbag.

"Except she didn't sell them," I said. "She kept them. Unless there were more things, besides the necklace and the book, that we don't know about."

"More likely she just didn't need to sell them," Percy said with a shrug. "Just like she didn't really need to steal jewelry. Roderick's family did take care of her, and she had plenty of money."

I thought of Mrs. B patting my hand when I'd said something similar. *You can always use more money, dear.*

I shook my head. "She was wearing the necklace when she died. Which would suggest she was using it, or at least that it was important to her."

Which would, in turn, suggest that Edith Baird was indeed a witch. Was that why she'd hired Tilly "Lester" in the first place? Had she known who Tilly really was?

"And the necklace was still on her when her killer buried her," I went on. "They couldn't have known how valuable it was, or they would've taken it. And obviously they didn't get the book, either. I guess that would eliminate Lester Mistmantle. He'd have wanted that stuff back."

"Her murder probably had nothing to do with that stuff," said Percy. "Just like Barbara's probably didn't. You know it's entirely possible this weird witchy side thing is just that: a side thing."

I rolled my eyes at him. "You don't really believe that."

"No?"

"Come on. A *stolen magic necklace*? It's definitely related."

"Okay. How?"

"Still working on that." I chewed at my thumbnail, replaying our conversation with Autumn Trelayne. She'd ended it by giving us her card, and urging us to please call her if there was anything at all she could do to help us locate the Mistmantle items. She was definitely eager. And she was an expert on this witch stuff; she could fill in blanks that I never could.

But I had a feeling Percy would laugh at any suggestion that she could actually help. "You really think they're crazy?"

"Who? The witches?"

"The Trelaynes, specifically. Autumn didn't seem crazy, did she?"

"Well, either she's crazy, or she actually casts magic spells, so." He tossed one hand, by way of finishing his sentence for him.

"You were kind of mean to her."

"I was not mean!" He glanced at me, genuinely surprised. "At worst, it was lighthearted teasing. She told me to treat it like a joke, so I did. Seemed to suit us both. I was just being funny."

I snorted. "Funny, or flirty?"

His laugh was slightly exasperated. "You just said I was mean. Now I was flirting? You think I flirt by being mean?"

I pretended to consider this. "Well, your first words to me were a scolding for being pretty."

He took my hand, then lifted it to his lips to kiss it. "Well, you deserved it. You were the prettiest woman I ever saw up close. What can I say, you had me flustered."

This was baldly untrue. The man had dated actresses. But I wasn't above accepting a sweet-hearted lie. I took my hand back so I could squeeze his knee. "Autumn Trelayne is very pretty."

"Is she? I couldn't really see the pretty around all that"—he gestured at his face— "crazy."

"Percy!"

"What?" The line between his brows suggested a concern that I might be the real crazy person in this scenario. "Are you really worried I was flirting with her? Because I would never do that. Not, you know, in *front* of you."

Ha, ha. I smacked his leg. "I'm not worried you were flirting with her. I'm worried you're dismissing her so easily."

"As opposed to what? Not dismissing her?" The exasperated laugh made an encore, by not-so-popular demand. "Minerva Biggs, please tell me this isn't your way of confessing that you believe in magic."

"No! Not really."

"Not *really*?"

"What do you mean, *confessing*?" I asked at the same time. "Like it would be some shameful secret? Need I remind you that not even a year ago you were telling me all about how Molly Towe laid a curse on the Howell family?"

"Yeah, in a quaint, local color kind of way." Percy huffed. "That kind of thing is fun to talk about, I guess, but you didn't believe it any more than I did."

"No. Not really."

"There's that *not really* again."

"I don't believe in witchcraft," I said firmly. Of course I didn't. Not in the sense of waving wands and conjuring fire, anyway. But that didn't seem to be the kind of witchcraft Autumn Trelayne had been talking about, either.

"Well, thank heavens for that," Percy said.

"But I believe in things we can't explain. You'd be a fool not to. They're all around you."

"That's not the same as magic."

"No?"

"No. They're just things we haven't found the logical explanation for *yet*." He shifted in his seat, and I suddenly realized that this wasn't a lighthearted conversation we were having. He looked genuinely uncomfortable.

"What is up with you?" I asked. "Why is this such a big deal?"

"Because! I thought we were"—he flicked his hand off the wheel—"you know."

"I don't know. If I knew, I wouldn't be asking."

"On the same page. With stuff."

"What stuff?" I laughed. "You thought our position on *witchcraft* was the same? And that's important to you?"

"Of course it's important!"

"Because it comes up so often?"

"Not in everyday stuff, no, but ..." Another shift in his seat. "I mean ..."

"What, Percy? What do you mean?"

"Is this the kind of cr—*stuff* you're going to teach our kids?"

I stiffened. This was the first time these hypothetical kids had been mentioned, by either of us. "Well, I guess I ... I mean, we'd talk about that, if we ... we'd decide together what ..."

"Yeah, that's what I'm doing. Talking about it."

"Does it have to be now? I wasn't aware we had kids. Have you impregnated me without my knowledge?"

For once, he was the one giving me the look that said I wasn't funny. "You've got to talk about this stuff. You don't want some crackpot raising—"

"Some *crackpot*? Did you just call me a crackpot?"

"No! I just meant, you know, you have to work these things out. In advance." He took my hand again, and this time the squeeze felt almost desperate. "If you're thinking about a future."

There it was. My opening. He'd brought it up first. All I had to do was say, *And you've been giving this future serious thought, have you?* And then, *Why yes, I have too. And I'm happy to disavow witchcraft, by the way, if that's*

THE GUEST IS HISTORY

a dealbreaker. It wasn't like I had any particular attachment to the idea.

But Plant chose that moment to get up and shake, sending a substantial string of drool flying onto the back of Percy's neck. There were the exclamations of disgust and the cleanup to deal with, and by the time all that was done his phone was buzzing with a call from Elaine, and then my phone was buzzing. The message that popped up on my screen was—almost—enough to drive the other stuff out of my mind.

"What's that face?" Percy asked, after he'd put off Elaine with the excuse that he was driving, and a promise to call her back.

"I've got a message from one of the Jane Weavers." I sat up straighter. "It's *the* Jane Weaver. Jane-Ann. I found the right one."

"Relative of Edith's, right?"

"Yeah, she confirms she's Clara Cotswold's great-great-granddaughter. That would make her Edith's great-great-niece. No. Three times great?" For someone as into genealogy as I'd become, I still got inordinately confused by the great math and the cousin math. "Whatever. She wants to know why I'm asking." I glanced up at Percy, suddenly nervous. "What should I say?"

"I don't know, the truth?"

"Right. I guess that can't hurt." I looked around at the scenery flying by. "How close are we to the hotel? Because if it's going to be a while you'll have to pull over, I can't message her while we're going, I'll get carsick. And it can't really wait, she's five hours ahead, or whatever it is. If I don't answer her until later she might not be around."

Percy's lips twitched as he kissed my hand again, a sure sign that I'd inadvertently started talking very fast, which he always seemed to find cute. "We're almost there."

I waited until I was sitting at the bottom of the nice, stationary bed at our hotel before engaging in a long back-and-forth with Jane-Ann Weaver, while Percy called his sister back. Jane-Ann was fascinated by the story of Edith's bones being discovered, and the suspicion of foul play, and was quite happy to help. She didn't personally have any photographs of Edith, but said she was pretty sure one of the older generation would have something, and that she'd get back to me.

Meanwhile, I started digging into the Mistmantles that very night. And every night after work for the next week, while Percy, still hiding from Baird House, worked late or took Plant for long walks.

I looked first not for Tilly but for her brother; military records were a great source of information, and men were usually easier to find in general. *History* was, in many ways, still very much *his*. I found a Lester Mistmantle who'd died at the Second Battle of the Marne in 1918. Working backward from there, I was able to confirm that he was the Lester I was looking for. He was the last surviving member of his family, having lost his sole remaining sibling, Matilda, in 1911.

Matilda had died in Italy—no word on why she was there, or with whom—at the age of nineteen. The cause of death was supposedly scarlet fever, which while not impossible was a red flag. As far as I knew, scarlet fever typically struck younger children. Further evidence that Matilda had faked her death, taken an assumed name, and considering the *Titanic* passenger list had her listed as twenty-one, chosen a slightly different date of birth, all to mask her true identity.

Edith Cotswold had married Roddy Baird in Italy in 1912, just after the turn of the year. Matilda might have met her there, either before or after the marriage. Maybe she became Edith's maid as a means of getting back to the United States. Or maybe they were friends, and the lady's maid thing was all part of the ruse.

As to why Tilly would have done all that, I could only speculate, and I had very little to go on. According to Autumn, the Mistmantles had been into some not-very-nice stuff. Maybe she'd been on the run.

Mostly this raised more questions than it answered, and brought me no closer to first, why Edith had taken Tilly's things; second, why Edith had been struck in the head and buried under a tree; and third, by whom.

And fourth, what all or any of that had to do with the death of Barbara Hingley. It didn't seem like Ruby and the rest of Bryd Hollow's finest had gotten any further with Barbara's murder than I had with Edith's. Kim was still insinuating—as often as possible—that some mysterious Tybryd staff member had done the deed to steal the watch and other antiques.

For all I knew, she was right. As Percy and I had already discussed, the list of people who'd known about the watch was probably pretty long.

That watch was worth a lot. Basil's guess was several

thousand on its own, but it might sell for ten times that —or more—if some *Titanic* enthusiast decided it counted as an artifact. Still, even then, I wasn't sure it was worth enough to kill a woman for.

Then again, maybe the murderer hadn't meant to kill the woman at all. Maybe they'd only been trying to steal it, and Barbara had interrupted them.

I finally got some answers at the end of that week, but they were answers I already knew: lab results had come back at last, and confirmed (or at least very strongly suggested) that the skeleton was Barbara Hingley's grandmother. In light of the fact that her maternal grandmother was already accounted for and buried in Georgia, paired with the fact that the bones had been buried with Roderick's watch, the powers that be officially declared the skeleton to be that of Edith Baird.

Kim delivered this news to me personally. I'd gone out to lunch with Snick, and dropped by Baird House to say hello to Mrs. B on my way back. I found her in the sitting room with her houseguest, and so was obliged to say hello to both of them whether I liked it or not.

"So that's two women in my family Tybryd has killed," Kim said with a sniff, when she'd finished her brief update. "Thank goodness I'm going home next week, or I could be next."

I couldn't say my true response to that out loud, so I just mumbled something about being sure she was glad it was resolved.

"I'll be having a joint service for both of them, at home." Kim reached across the couch to pat Mrs. B's arm. "Bessie has offered to host it all. I'll admit I think

THE GUEST IS HISTORY

that's only appropriate, considering, so I agreed to let her."

She always called Mrs. B "Bessie." She seemed to think it marked her as an insider, when really it did the opposite. As for her "letting" Mrs. B host, this didn't surprise me in the least. I assumed *host* was code for *plan, pay, and do all the work for.*

A suspicion confirmed by Kim's next words. "She said you'll help, since you used to be an event planner. I'll email you a list of my ideas."

Mrs. B's cheeks went a little pink. I wondered whether she'd been hitting the wine already. Not that I'd have blamed her. "Well, I was going to *ask* you, of course, Minerva."

Was she? That would've been progress for her, if so. I gave both women my brightest smile. "Of course, I'd love to help."

Mrs. B murmured her thanks, while Kim waved my agreement away like it was a given.

"I told Bessie you would. Obviously the whole family will want to come, given their"—Kim gave a dainty little cough—"*involvement*, and I figured you'd want a reason to tag along with Percy."

I was more surprised that she wanted Percy there than I was by her assumption that I would want to "tag along." But I supposed I shouldn't have been, considering the level of snobbery and social climbing she'd displayed so far. I imagined her top priority was showing her friends and neighbors how very close she was with the Tybryd Bairds.

At least I managed to hold all my sighs until I got

into my car, at which point I heaved several in a row. I did not have time to plan a double funeral—in Georgia, no less.

But I had to admit, I wouldn't mind seeing Edith laid to rest at last. If only I could figure out who killed her, maybe she could even rest in peace.

Besides, I had a feeling that if I'd said no, the task would've fallen to Snick, and he was apt to have a nervous breakdown if that happened. It was difficult to say whether Kim's stay in Bryd Hollow was more of a trial for him, or for Percy. Although Snick had expressed some regret that Tabitha couldn't stay on. Apparently she spent most of her time in the kitchen or upstairs on the staff level, which he considered neglectful on Kim's part. And she was by all accounts a very nice cat.

Chapter Ten

WITHOUT WAITING for an answer to her knock, Mrs. B pulled open my office door with a flourish, like she was presenting herself to a cheering crowd on her front lawn. I'd specifically asked for that door to open outward to save space, but I supposed indulging her penchant for a dramatic entrance was just as good a reason.

"Oh!" She clasped her hands to her chest. "What a *darling* little office! Isn't it just *darling*? But what am I doing here?"

It was well she should ask; she'd never set foot in Tail-bryd before, and probably never thought to. She'd washed her hands of the family business decades ago, if she'd ever been involved at all. But I'd called both her and Percy urgently, telling them we had to have an emergency meeting right away, and that I'd explain when they got here.

I needed to talk to them both—away from Baird House, where Kim might overhear.

I certainly needed to talk to *somebody*. And Plant just

wasn't as scandalized by what I'd discovered that morning as I needed him to be.

Percy hurried in a couple minutes later, asking the same question his mother had (without the exclamations of admiration for my darling office). I closed the door, then gestured for them both to sit at my desk, where I'd already put an extra chair. The room really wasn't big enough for the two Bairds, me, and Plant (especially when the latter was excited to see Percy, and bouncing around like a fool), but that was okay. I needed them sitting close together, so they could both see my laptop screen as clearly as possible.

As soon as I got Plant settled down, I leaned between Percy and Mrs. B long enough to pull up a photo. "Jane-Ann Weaver sent that photograph of Edith Cotswold she promised me. I just got it a couple hours ago. That's her. Jane-Ann's great-aunt says it's from 1910."

"She's pretty," said Mrs. B.

"Little horsey around the mouth," Percy added.

Both things were true, but I wasn't here to critique Edith's looks. I leaned over again and clicked my mouse, tiling the windows so they could see the picture of the midsummer party side-by-side with Edith's face. "She isn't there."

Percy frowned at me over his shoulder. "What?"

"Look for yourselves. Zoom in and out. Take your time."

I'd certainly taken mine. After weeks of anticipation, I'd been so excited to finally see Edith's face, and more than that, to see it when she was among the Bairds. I'd scoured the midsummer photo for a match, starting with the four we'd narrowed it down to, then studying every face—even the men's—as I got more and more desperate to find her.

I wanted to see her expression at that party. Had she been happy, in her last days of life? Nervous? Scared? Did she resent this new family of hers for their snobbishness? Or did she yearn for their approval?

Well, none of those things. Because Edith Cotswold Baird wasn't there.

"So ... they took the photo *after* she disappeared?" Mrs. B asked. "That seems a little bit *rude*, doesn't it? Or I don't know, just in poor *taste*."

"I don't think that's it," I said. "We already know how into their event photos Emily and Alistair Baird were. Everybody is always in them. I'm sure they made sure by taking the photograph at the beginning. Like they did with the first ball."

I realized Mrs. B's explanation was the first one that would occur to most people: Edith simply wasn't around when the photograph was taken. It needn't have been after her disappearance. Maybe she'd just gone to the bathroom.

But Edith's absence, and the way Emily had been about her pictures, and the fact that Edith not only had Tilly's things, but was wearing one of those things when she died—it was all mounting up to another possibility. One that was, as far as I was concerned, equally likely. (Okay, as far as I was concerned it was actually *more* likely, but that was mainly because my imagination had seized on it so hard.)

Percy looked back at me again, eyes narrowed. "You

don't think she's Edith, do you?"

"Wait, you've lost me," said Mrs. B.

"That's because we haven't told you about the witch thing," I said.

"Because it's too crazy to bother you with," Percy added.

"*Witch* thing?" Mrs. B turned sideways in her chair, so she could see us both. "Of *course* I need to hear a *witch* thing!"

"It's about that book that Barbara brought, and Edith's necklace," I said. "Apparently they're some kind of witchcraft paraphernalia. The person who identified them for us recognized the bear thing as a family emblem. We think they belonged to somebody named Tilly Mistmantle.

"*Mistmantle!* That's a fine, spooky name for a witch!" Mrs. B's eyes danced with laughter. I guessed she wasn't any more of a believer than her son. Not that I wasn't a skeptic myself. (Mostly.) "Isn't it *spooky*?"

"It's a little spooky," I agreed. "Tilly was Edith's lady's maid, and supposedly died on the *Titanic*."

I looked from her to Percy. "Here's the thing. I've seen John Baird for myself. Actually, you have too. Kim brought some more pictures with her, paper ones. We saw them at lunch that day, do you remember?"

He shrugged, brow furrowed. "Kind of. Is it important?"

I couldn't fault his hazy memory. It had been a quick thing, just before Kim and Barbara left for the hotel. I'd nearly forgotten, myself. Especially with everything that had happened the next day. "The paper ones are only important to make the point that the first one I saw, the digital one, wasn't doctored or anything. Plus John was a World War II vet, and he was in uniform in one of them. So that confirms the timeframe. So we've definitely seen John, the real John."

"Okay," said Percy. "And?"

"And he might have been Roderick's twin rather than his son. In other words, Barbara's father was definitely a Baird. And therefore so was she."

Mrs. B blinked at me. "Was there ever any question they were Bairds?" She pressed her hand to her chest. "I never heard *those* sorts of rumors about Edith. Not *before* Roddy died."

I pointed at her. "Exactly. There *wasn't* ever any question they were Bairds. We identified Edith's bones on the basis that she was related to Barbara, and we knew Barbara was a Baird." I spread my hands. "It didn't occur to us to question whether she was a Cotswold."

"So you think Edith was actually Tilly. That she switched somehow." Percy swiveled in his chair to better face me, then seemed to realize that he was sitting while a lady—his lady, no less—was standing, and shot up like the seat had shocked him. "Sit."

Plant immediately sat, which made me laugh. "I'm fine."

Percy still wouldn't sit while I was standing. He leaned back against the desk instead, drumming his fingers against it. "But you're making a point of emphasizing that her baby was Roderick's. So you're suggesting Roderick Baird impregnated both his wife and her maid?"

"I can't speak to whether his wife was pregnant," I said. "But it's hardly outside the realm of possibility that he impregnated her maid. The Bairds of that generation were womanizers. You've told me so yourself."

Mrs. B gave the rare snicker. "The Bairds of most generations are womanizers."

"Yeah," said Percy, "but he was a *newlywed*."

Mrs. B reached over to pat her son's hand. "Oddly enough, sweetheart, of the two of us I'm the one more familiar with this particular family tradition." She flapped her hand at him. "Unless you've been womanizing. And I don't want to hear about *that*."

"I have not been womanizing." Percy gave me a little sideways smile, just the one dimple. "I haven't even been flirting."

"Well then, I'm the authority," Mrs. B said. "And I agree with Minerva. It's certainly *possible* that Roddy had an affair with his wife's maid."

"So let's stipulate," I said, "just for the sake of argument, that Roderick was having a fling on the side with Tilly. He boards the *Titanic* with both women. Tragedy strikes."

"Technically, iceberg strikes," Percy said with a chuckle.

"No, technically the ship strikes the iceberg. The passengers aren't sure what's going on. They don't think the ship will sink—that's pretty much unthinkable, at least for a while yet—but they do know something is wrong. And at some point Roderick realizes that it's something deadly, because he asks to get in the lifeboat."

"With his *wife*," Percy interjected. "Who you're

saying is actually Tilly. So assuming he can tell the difference between his wife and his mistress, he's intentionally swapping them. Why would he do that? Both women could have gotten onto a boat, right? Women and children first? And Tilly was traveling first class with her employer."

"Sure," I said, "but you're assuming whoever came up with this plan was interested in keeping Edith alive. The fact that Roderick was going along with it doesn't mean it was his idea."

"Ah. So it was the"—Percy wiggled his fingers in the air—"dark magic."

"Seems logical to assume it was Tilly's plan, considering she was the one who really benefitted from it." I looked over his shoulder at my laptop, where the midsummer party photo was still up. I was now sure one of those faces belonged to Matilda Mistmantle.

I'd been looking for Edith on a summer day. Now my imagination reached for Tilly on a cold night instead.

"She was in Lifeboat 10," I murmured, to myself rather than Percy and Mrs. B.

But it was a small room, and Percy heard me clearly enough to tease me. "You actually know which lifeboat she was in."

I shrugged. "You can find that stuff. There are records. Especially of first-class people."

"Is it significant?"

"It was one of the last boats to leave. Only half an hour before it was all over. The ship was listing by then."

She would have been freezing. Probably scared. There would have been a lot of confusion. Families being separated. Women and children—and probably a few men—weeping and wailing.

"So *now* they realize the ship is going to sink," Percy said.

"I'm sure they do." I cleared my throat, forcing myself back to the present. "But Tilly must have figured it out much earlier. It was 11:40 when the ship hit the iceberg. Oh, don't give me that face, I obviously reviewed all of this when I started researching Edith. The point is, there were about two hours between the collision and the launch of Lifeboat 10. Plenty of time for Tilly to ascertain the situation and get up to no good. Maybe she overheard somebody talking early on. Or maybe she had some kind of witchy premonition."

"So what did she do?" Mrs. B was hanging on my words like this was an event I'd actually witnessed. I appreciated the support. "Trap the real Edith in her closet and take her clothes?"

"Maybe," I said. Hey, it was as good a theory as any. And we would never know for sure. "I doubt Edith just passively agreed to the swap, so either Tilly or Roderick must have done something to her. Drugged her, knocked her out. Maybe just killed her outright."

"But *why*?" Mrs. B gestured at Percy. "You just said Tilly could have gotten onto a boat *herself*. There was no reason to pretend to be somebody else."

"Because it was an opportunity," I said. "Maybe Tilly hated Edith, or maybe she just liked Edith's life better, and this was her chance to take it. She'd already assumed another identity once. She must have had a reason.

Maybe she was on the run from her brother, or some enemy."

"She was a dark wizard," Percy stage-whispered. "Who knows why villains do what they do."

Mrs. B pursed her lips at him. "But why would *Roddy* go along? He must have loved his own *wife*, at least a little. He'd just married her! There is a very big difference between cheating on her and sentencing her to *death*."

Maybe Tilly bewitched him.

"Because Tilly was carrying his child," Percy said. Okay, I had to admit his answer was more likely. "His *only* child—then and maybe ever, since he wasn't sure he was going to survive the night."

I nodded, my mind traveling back to that cold, and now horridly sloping, deck. The slope is getting steeper. Children are crying. Everybody is yelling. Things that should not be cracking and groaning and popping are starting to crack and groan and pop.

In just twenty minutes, the lights will go out. There will be only darkness and icy water and screams. And then worse—silence.

"He tries to go home with her," I said. "But when he's denied, he gives her the watch, and Edith's ring. And not, you'll notice, a photo from their wedding, or anything that could prove to his family—who have never met his wife, and only know of her by telegram—that she's really Edith."

I spread my hands, resting my case. "Because she's not."

Percy ran his hand through his hair. He looked like

he might have just come back from 1912, too. "He needed to make sure his kid would be raised as a legitimate one."

"And inherit everything," I added. "His name, his fortune. Tilly's son would be his only legacy." I looked at Mrs. B. "I suppose that's what he sacrificed his wife for."

"Well!" she said. "That is quite a *story*! And it sounds possible. It all fits." She turned to Percy. "Doesn't it sound *possible*?"

"Wait." I held up my hand. "Before you answer that, there's more."

I'd managed, after much digging, to find a photo of Lester Mistmantle's military unit. I leaned over the desk and pulled it up. "I don't have a picture of Tilly, but that's her brother Lester on the far right. Second one in. There could be a resemblance to Barbara there, couldn't there? The shape of the jaw, and the wide mouth?"

Both Percy and Mrs. B squinted at the photo.

"Maybe!" Mrs. B gave me an encouraging nod. I suspected she enjoyed the thought of Barbara and Kim coming from witch stock.

Percy looked a little more skeptical. Possibly because if you zoomed the photo in far enough to actually see Lester's face, it got way too blurry to draw any conclusions about his bone structure.

All right, fine, I was reaching.

But everything else added up. I straightened up and moved back from the desk, stopping short of stepping on Plant's foot. "John was definitely Roderick's son, which means Roderick was definitely Barbara's grandfather. And we know for sure from the lab results that the woman in the ground was Barbara's grandmother. Ergo, the woman murdered at the midsummer party is the woman who had Roderick Baird's baby. And now we know from the photo Jane-Ann sent me that Edith Cotswold was not at that party."

"We don't know for sure that the skeleton was murdered at the party," Percy pointed out. "We just assumed that because we thought it was Edith. And we don't know Edith wasn't at the party, either. We only know she's not in the picture."

I gave him my teacher look, which I'd kept in good form, by way of conveying that he was being difficult. "We thought it was Edith because she had Roderick's watch, which 'Edith' always carried. And because the dating on the bones matches up. And because Roderick Baird died in April of 1912, so nobody else was running around having his babies and then getting murdered at Tybryd."

I had no hard rebuttal—yet—to the possibility that Edith simply hadn't been there for the group photograph, so I pretended I hadn't heard that part. Instead I took a page from Mrs. B's book, and resorted to italics. "Obviously I can't *prove* all of this. And I might have some of the details wrong. But I *know* that the Edith who came off Lifeboat 10 is not the same Edith who got on the *Titanic*."

And I did know it. Down to my own bones. I was no longer—and in fact never had been—investigating Edith Baird's death.

I was investigating Tilly Mistmantle's.

Chapter Eleven

NOTHING about the family legend suggested that anybody had been anything short of thoroughly fooled by Tilly's ruse. There was never so much as a whisper, as far as I could find, that she'd been an imposter. And if the other attendees of the midsummer party all thought she was Edith, their motives, means, and opportunities for her murder remained the same. A jealous wife whose husband she'd had a fling with. An angry husband whose advances she'd rejected. Somebody who just didn't like her (which, by the sound of it, was pretty much everybody).

But the mysterious stranger was another matter. If Edith was actually Tilly, it seemed to me that he became a lot less mysterious. Not that I knew his name or anything —but I was fairly certain I could list his occupation as *blackmailer*.

Given the theft, it made sense. Roderick's fortune had been modest in comparison to his Uncle Alistair's. Tilly probably didn't own anything as valuable as the jewelry she stole. So why settle for the smaller prize, when you might be able to force Tilly to access the larger one for you?

Maybe it was here in Bryd Hollow that the black-mailer had discovered Tilly, or maybe he'd followed her here. Either way, he was seen approaching her at night, making his demand. So Tilly brought him the jewelry, hoping it would be enough.

It wasn't. She knew he would never let her go. The meeting got confrontational. There was a struggle. Maybe Tilly even tried a little witchcraft—she was wearing the focus, after all. Wasn't that supposed to help her cast spells?

If so, it didn't work. Tilly ended up dead.

Or better yet, considering the location of the head trauma, maybe there was no struggle at all. Maybe the blackmailer took his payment, thanked her very much, then as soon as she turned away, knocked her on the head and killed her. Maybe so he could never be identified. That seemed to have worked; he never had been. Edith—Tilly—was conveniently blamed for the theft, and off he went.

Or maybe he just killed her because he didn't like her, and wanted her dead in addition to wanting to be paid. According to Autumn, Tilly was, as Percy was so fond of putting it, an evil wizard. That didn't need to actually be true. The killer just needed to believe it was true.

And there was evidence, for the evil part anyway: she'd killed Edith. Maybe he found out, and killed her for revenge. Or simple justice.

Or maybe Edith wasn't the only one she'd killed.

Maybe the blackmailer was whomever she'd been running from when she shed her identity the first time. Maybe he caught up with her at last.

That was a whole lot of maybes. As ever, the frustrating truth was that I could tell myself any story that caught my fancy, and declare the case closed any time I wanted. But I'd probably never really know what happened to Tilly Mistmantle. Or to Edith Baird, for that matter. All I had was conjecture.

Still, amongst all that conjecture there was one thing I could—and was determined to—prove. Which was how Percy and I came to be in Ruby Walker's office, the day after I got Edith's picture from Jane-Ann.

I explained why I had reason to believe that the woman they'd just identified as Edith Cotswold Baird was actually an imposter. Mostly explained. I told her that the medallion the skeleton was wearing was a family emblem that led us to identify Edith's maid. And I told her the main thing, which was that the real Edith wasn't in the midsummer photograph.

But I left out all the witchcraft stuff. I had no doubt that if I went that far, Ruby's glasses would be obliged to slide so low on her nose to enable her power glare, they'd actually fall off her face.

Ruby was, as usual, not amused. "Occam's razor," she said. "The simplest explanation is almost always the right one. In this case, that would be that Edith went to pee and missed the picture. Happens with bridesmaids all the time, I don't see why this should be any different."

Percy gave me a look and tossed his hand, as if to say *There you are*. He'd told me on the way over that she would say that. Which, as far as I was concerned, did not make him a fizzing prognosticator. Of course she was going to say that.

"I'm aware that's the most obvious answer," I said. "Which is why I need to prove that it's not the right one. Jane-Ann Weaver—that's the lady who sent me Edith's picture—has generously agreed to a DNA test. I want to test her DNA against the bones. If there's no biological relationship between Jane-Ann and the woman you've identified as Edith, then that woman was not a Cotswold."

Maybe I couldn't prove she was Tilly, but I could at least prove she wasn't Edith. At which point, the Tilly part seemed like a safe conclusion, considering the circumstantial evidence pointing in that direction.

Ruby pursed her lips. "And you're asking me about this instead of Kim Hollander because ..."

"Because Kim isn't the most helpful and cooperative person." I paused for Ruby's snort before going on. I had a feeling she had even more experience with that than I did. "And she's already been known to get touchy about her lineage. I don't want to tell her about any of this until I have proof. So we were kind of hoping maybe you could lend us the sample the county already has. Since they're done with it."

Ruby leaned forward in her chair and clasped her hands on top of her desk, pinning not me but Percy with her stare. "And you're here as what, the money?"

Percy bit back a laugh. "Yep, pretty much. My family is willing to pay for a private test. And unlike Minerva, we must have some rights here, right? I mean the person you've identified as Edith Baird is our family, and her bones were found on our property. If we want to dispute the county's findings and say she's *not* Edith—at our own expense—isn't that an option for us?"

"That's an interesting question," said Ruby. She did not, in fact, look particularly interested. She looked like she was losing patience, which was faster than usual. And she kept looking down at her phone, like she was checking the time. "Believe it or not, I'm not up on all the ins and outs of dealing with dusty old bones. Families can request things like autopsies, at their own expense, if they believe it's necessary and the county disagrees. You could probably do something along those lines. But I doubt you'd be able to do it without a court order, or the permission of Edith's closest kin."

She waved a hand at me. "Which would be Kim."

I bit my lip. "Right."

There was a knock on Ruby's door, immediately followed by Roark's head popping in. "Asheville PD is setting up now. They're going live in a few."

Asheville PD? What was Ruby doing with the Asheville PD?

"Thank you." Ruby put her palms on top of her desk and stood. When she saw me open my mouth, she glared me into silence.

But then her eyebrows shot up. "I just thought of something. I might be able to help you."

"How so?" I asked.

"If you can use the bones to check for a bio relationship with your friend Jane-Ann, you should be able to

THE GUEST IS HISTORY

use Barbara's DNA to do the same thing, right? If the grandmother is related, then the granddaughter will be."

"Yyyyes," I said slowly. I thought the test might be less conclusive, on account of the Cotswold DNA being more diluted in Barbara than it would be in Edith (if she were actually Edith). But that was coming from a position of knowing absolutely nothing about it. Possibly less than nothing, since a TV education usually resulted in negative knowledge.

Ruby offered me a rare smile. Rare to me, anyway. "I have a signed release from Barbara, allowing the use of her DNA sample in any way necessary to assist with the identification of our Jane Doe's skeleton. Since you're disputing that identification, and Barbara's DNA would help resolve the matter, I would think this situation would qualify. And as far as I know, the release is still binding after her death."

"In other words," said Percy, "a judge or next of kin would have to give consent on Edith's behalf, but not on Barbara's. Because we already have Barbara's consent."

"That about sums it up. If we both fill out a few forms, we should be able to get your private test approved. Without having to notify anybody else. It might not be *strictly* the correct process, but the victim whose identity you're disputing has been dead for over a hundred years. As long as there's paperwork to cover their butts, the county won't care." Ruby walked to her door, which Roark had left open, and gestured for us to precede her into the small police station beyond. "I trust my helping you out will mean you won't bug me anymore. Kind of like bribing an officer, but in reverse."

I narrowed my eyes at her. Ruby Walker, possibly stretching the rules to help us? That was definitely the clincher. "Why are you trying to get rid of us so fast?"

She sighed. "Because I have things to do. I am working today, if you hadn't noticed."

"Yeah, but the only big, serious case you have is Barbara's. You wouldn't be working with the Asheville police on busting a traffic offender." I pointed at her. "Something is going on with the case, that you want us out of the station for."

Ruby considered me for a few seconds, chewing the inside of her cheek. "I *did* want you out of the station for it, because you're a couple of insufferable busybodies." She flicked her hand for us to follow her. "But now that you mention it, maybe you two can help."

"Help with what?" I asked. She was leading us toward the little back rooms that, in my experience, didn't mean anything fun.

"A woman contacted an antiques dealer over in Asheville a few days ago about the watch. What she didn't know was that this guy is one of Basil's golfing buddies."

I frowned. The woman part didn't surprise me; Barbara had been a slight, elderly woman, and she'd been hit from behind. It would hardly have taken a big burly man to overpower her. But the golfing buddy thing did surprise me. "That was clumsy of her. Way to not do your homework."

"Clumsiness gets them caught almost as often as sheer stupidity," Ruby said with a shrug. "The dealer told Basil, and Basil told us."

"And now you're setting up a sting?" Percy chuckled, like that was a joke, but Ruby nodded.

She stopped outside one of the interview rooms. "In here."

There was a very large monitor set up on the table. Roark sat in front of it, another chair—presumably for Ruby—beside him.

"We got the dealer to insist they make the exchange in person," said Ruby, "which isn't a suspicious request, considering we're talking about ten grand."

"Ten grand?" I interrupted. It was a lot of money, but in my opinion a bit of a lowball for that particular watch. With time and patience, the killer could have gotten much more. "Guess she's getting anxious to move it?"

Roark nodded at me over his shoulder. "Either she's afraid she'll get caught with it, or she really needs the money."

"Asheville PD have agreed to help us," Ruby said. "They'll grab her when she comes in, that simple."

I gestured at the monitor. "So what's all this then, if it's so simple?"

"Given the high chance the killer has some connection to Bryd Hollow, I didn't want any of our people anywhere near that store. So the dealer's wearing a body cam. Which is where you two come in. Maybe you'll recognize someone I wouldn't."

I glanced at Percy, who flinched a little bit. She meant, of course, that we might recognize a Tybryd employee. He was still really hoping that wasn't where Barbara's case would end up.

"Does Kim know about this?" I asked.

Ruby shook her head as she sat down. "Not yet. She's still a suspect in the case."

Roark looked back at me again. "Did you want the chair?"

"Do not give her the chair!" Ruby smacked his arm. "There's a time to be a gentleman, Roark, but while you're doing your job is not that time. I need you front and center."

"I'm fine standing," I assured him.

"Aren't *we* suspects?" Percy asked.

Ruby waved this away. "Nah, your alibis checked out."

"You were sitting in the booth next to mine at Cullen's half the night," Roark said with a laugh. "I'm about as reliable a witness as it gets." He nodded at me. "And your neighbor remembered you guys walking Plant later."

"Besides," said Ruby, "neither of you qualifies for motive. Murder is always love or money. Bonus points if it's both."

She made a shushing noise, as if we'd been the ones who were talking. Roark snapped to attention like a soldier and turned back to the monitor. The screen flashed, then an image of a counter in what I assumed was the antiques store came up. I could hear a man breathing.

"He sells mostly high-end stuff," said Ruby. "Including art. Does a lot of auctions."

"Sounds like buying stolen property from murderers

is new to him, though," said Roark. "The Asheville guy I talked to this morning said he was nervous."

"Let's hope he isn't so nervous he tips the killer off," I said. I was feeling nervous myself, even though I was miles away and powerless to do anything short of telling Ruby whether I recognized a face. I hadn't yet adjusted to the idea of what was happening—an actual *sting operation*, right here in Bryd Hollow. Well, in Asheville. But also in Bryd Hollow.

Were we really about to see Barbara's killer?

It seemed so abrupt. But then I guessed it would, to an outsider. It probably seemed like a long time coming to Roark and Ruby and the rest of the police.

The perspective of the camera was odd. It reminded me of looking through a keyhole. I could only vaguely see the shop door when it opened and closed again. But I could see well enough to note that the person who came in was a young man in a ratty coat.

He was fidgeting as he walked up to the counter and laid a manila envelope on it. The envelope wasn't padded, or at least not sufficiently to muffle the soft clank as he set it down.

"You have one for me?" he asked. He sounded nervous, too.

So this was definitely the exchange, not some random customer. Which meant the woman was at least smart enough not to come in person. Ruby muttered something under her breath. I had the sense it wasn't anything nice.

"I'm not sure." The antique dealer's hand came into

view, reaching for the envelope. "I was expecting a Mrs. Gochev."

"I don't know her name," the young man said. "She was Eastern European, though. She gave me two hundred bucks to come in here, give you this, and take an envelope from you back to her."

"Take it back to her where and when?" The dealer was pretty good at this. I heard the tear of paper—and then the watch slid out onto the counter. As far as I could see, it looked like the real thing.

"Honeybear's Cafe, in an hour." The young man tugged at the sleeves of his coat. "I'm not looking for trouble here. Can't we just keep this simple?"

"I'm afraid not," the dealer said.

As if on cue—well, probably actually on cue—a man and woman in street clothes came in and identified themselves as police officers. The young man swore, skittered toward the door like he might try to run, then stopped again. "I really don't want any trouble."

"Perfect!" the female officer said. "Neither do we. What's your name?"

"Carl."

"And how did you meet Mrs. Gochev, Carl?"

"I work at Honeybear's. She came in this morning."

"You'd never seen her before?"

"No."

"And she just trusted you to make this exchange without skimming a little off the top?"

He shrugged. "She knows where I work. Plus I wasn't supposed to open the envelope. I only get the other half of my money if it hasn't been opened."

The officer patted Carl's shoulder. "Sorry, Carl, but you won't be getting the other half anyway. But hey, at least you got the first half, right?"

Carl's face lit up. "I can keep it?"

There was nearly a half hour's confusion after that, before Ruby got off her phone and told us Carl was cooperating, and would meet Mrs. Gochev at Honeybear's as planned. There wouldn't be a camera this time, but we were welcome to wait anyway.

We did. She never showed.

She'd probably been watching the store (or the cafe, or both), and somehow figured out the police were there. They would watch Honeybear's for a few days, but I doubted they'd find her. It seemed Mrs. Gochev knew when to cut her losses.

The watch was recovered, but the killer was long gone.

Chapter Twelve

WE WERE DRIVING down to Georgia for the funeral services I'd so painstakingly planned when we got the call from the lab.

It was just Percy and me in the Jeep. Kim had asked me to leave Plant at home, and Elaine and Phil had decided to fly with Mrs B. (Which took at least as long, by the time you connected all the dots between the middle of nowhere in western North Carolina and the middle of nowhere in northern Georgia. Hence us skipping all that and driving.) So when I told Percy who was calling him, he told me to go ahead and answer it, and put it on speaker.

The call wasn't long. The upshot was: I was right. Edith Cotswold Baird was not, in fact, Edith Cotswold Baird.

Naturally, I felt vindicated by this overwhelming proof that I was the greatest detective since Poirot. And I wasn't above a little gloating. Maybe even a smirk. "So *now* do you believe me?"

Percy reached over and took my hand, looking more amused than humbled. "It wasn't that I didn't believe you. I paid for the test, didn't I?" Yes, he had. I'd offered —I wasn't making bad money, now that I was the director of something—but he'd refused. As usual. Always the gentleman, was Percy Baird. "I just didn't see the point in speculating about Tilly's murder until we knew for sure that it was Tilly who was murdered."

"I guess we still don't know for *sure*." I unwrapped a piece of taffy, handed it to Percy, then unwrapped one of my own. "This only proves that the bones aren't Edith's. But she was wearing Tilly's necklace. She passed Tilly's book down to her son. Who else would she be, if not Tilly?"

"Nobody," Percy agreed, the words a little garbled by the taffy. "The skeleton is definitely Tilly. This is as close to proving it as we'll ever get, probably, if Autumn was right and there are no Mistmantles left to beg for a test."

"Do you think Barbara knew? She was so weird about that book. I assume she knew what it was."

"Probably, but it's a big leap from *Grandma Edith left Dad a spellbook* to *Grandma Edith was actually a con artist named Tilly Mistmantle*. John was just a baby when Tilly died. She couldn't have told him anything."

"In which case, how did John or Barbara even figure out that the book was a spellbook?"

More importantly, if Barbara was a witch like her grandmother, did that have anything to do with her death? Or had it really been about the watch, after all? We were no closer to identifying the mysterious Mrs. Gochev. Carl had described her as being in her forties or fifties, short and heavyset with a heavy accent and a bit of a mustache—which described exactly nobody any of us knew. The watch had already been returned to Kim, having offered no evidence as to who'd taken it. Personally, I didn't think the ten thousand Mrs. Gochev had negotiated for it was worth risking a murder charge for, but people had been killed for less.

I chewed at my thumbnail. "What about Kim? Do we think she knows? About the witchcraft, at least?"

Percy shrugged, hands drumming against the wheel. "Guess we'll find out tomorrow."

I stared at him. "You can't think we should tell her about this at her mother's funeral. She's an awful person, but that seems exceptionally cold."

He glanced at me, brow knit. "It's not meant to be cold. It's"—he raised his fingers to make air quotes—"'Edith's' funeral, too. Obviously we have to tell Kim who she's burying. We can't keep that from her."

"Huh." I leaned my head against the back of the seat. "When you put it like that, I guess it's our duty."

We settled on telling Kim at the first opportunity to speak with her alone. And while we were at it, doing some subtle digging to find out what she knew about either her great-grandmother or her mother. And whether what she knew was more or different than what we knew.

Which was all well and good to decide on, but subtle digging wasn't a prominent part of my skill set. Or subtlety of any kind. And Percy was arguably worse.

Plus you had to take into account how thrown off

balance we were, when we showed up at the cemetery to find Autumn Trelayne there.

We were late, owing to my spending the past hour at Kim's house, wrangling the caterers. And making multiple calls to the florist, who'd apparently delivered a number of arrangements to Barbara's house rather than to either of the two places people were actually going to be memorializing Barbara. This was the sort of thing that happened when you planned an event from two states away, with nobody but Kim on the ground locally.

When we finally got to the cemetery where Barbara and Tilly were being put to rest in a small Hingley family mausoleum, the first thing I noticed was a stone angel standing guard over the door. I wondered how she would feel about a witch—or possibly two—taking up permanent residence in her domain. Autumn and her cousins seemed nice enough, and I had to assume there were good witches. But if my theories were even a quarter correct, Matilda Mistmantle had not been one of them.

No more than half a dozen live people could fit in the mausoleum, so the service was being held just outside. Percy and I hung back, hoping our tardiness wouldn't be noticed by anybody other than Mrs. B, who'd already given us a stern look. I didn't see Autumn until my mind began to wander about halfway through, when I started idly studying the older Hingley family headstones scattered around.

She was behind us, looking down and obviously reading the headstones, too. I did a double take, but really there was no mistaking that hair. My view of her must have been blocked when we arrived by the woman who'd just escorted her screaming toddler away.

Which conveniently left Autumn, Percy, and me pretty much alone back there. I took what I intended to be a couple of quiet, inconspicuous steps backward. There were enough people in front of me that I couldn't see the minister's face, and I hoped that meant he wouldn't see me, either.

Except the thing with cemeteries is, they're full of tripping hazards. I stumbled over a stone I hadn't seen over my shoulder, and nearly went down. A yelp of surprise escaped me before I could stop it.

Percy started toward me to try to steady me, but he would've been too late. A good thing—I guessed—that Autumn was there to take my arm and help me out.

The minister stopped talking. I cleared my throat and offered a no-doubt embarrassing apology that I mercifully forgot seconds after the words left my mouth. I hoped everybody else would forget too. Although judging by the look on Elaine's face, she'd be hanging on to that one for a while.

At least my faux pas had achieved one thing: distance. I tugged Autumn back a couple steps more for good measure, so we'd be out of earshot of everybody else, if we were quiet enough. Percy and I flanked her like a couple of guards. Or witch hunters, maybe.

"What are you doing here?" I whispered.

Apparently she didn't agree with my earshot calculation. She gestured for us to follow her around a tree, where we were largely out of sight as well. She still kept her voice down, though. "I was invited. I've been talking to Kim since that day you came to the store. Well, the day after, I think, by the time I tracked her down."

"How did you do that?" Percy asked. "We never told you her name."

Autumn huffed softly. "You told me yours. Witches have internet too, you know. Bit of a scandal on your hands there, huh?"

Percy's jaw worked a little. Autumn was clearly teasing—probably getting him back for the bad magic jokes—but it was still a sore subject. "So you somehow tracked down Kim's number and ... what?" he asked. "What were you talking to her about?"

"Considering there was a Mistmantle focus and spellbook in the family, I wanted to see if she had any other heirlooms she might be looking to sell."

"Did Kim know the spellbook and the focus were a spellbook and a focus?" I asked.

"Not that she'd admit," said Autumn. "I don't usually use the word *witchcraft* unless they do. I only told her I was an antiques dealer, and that I specialized in the sorts of things that had been stolen from her mother."

Percy raised a brow. "Stolen from her *murdered* mother. You somehow avoided her calling you a vulture and hanging up on you?"

Autumn shrugged, unperturbed as ever by Percy. "I'm a professional vulture. I'll admit it's the worst part of my job, but I'm pretty good at it."

"And then she just up and invited you to her mother's funeral?" Percy looked skeptical.

I couldn't say I blamed him. Kim could barely find basic manners for anybody, let alone somebody calling her just days after her mother was murdered, asking if she had any more obscure stuff that *wasn't* stolen that she might like to sell. Then again, Kim did have a keen interest in money.

Autumn waved a hand. "More or less. We got to chatting, and she invited me to come down and have a look through Barbara's attic before she closes up her house."

I heard voices from the other side of the tree, multiple people talking to each other. The service must have been over. I'd have to get back to Kim's house soon.

But at least it was safe to talk in normal voices now, because I had one other question for Autumn first. "Unrelated, but while I have you, do you have any resources that I don't, that might produce a photograph of Matilda Mistmantle?"

Autumn laughed. "And by *resources* you mean"—she wiggled her fingers in the air, looking more like Percy than she probably would have liked, if she'd known— "weird witch stuff?"

"Yeah, pretty much."

"I'm afraid not. Why do you ask?"

"Because I need a photograph to confirm she was at a house party at Tybryd in 1913."

Autumn frowned. "Where Edith died?"

I shook my head, hoping I didn't look too proud of myself. "Nope, where *Tilly* died. That wasn't Edith Baird we buried today. Edith died on the *Titanic*, and Tilly stole her identity."

Percy tapped my thigh, I guessed to warn me that in my enthusiasm for showing off my investigative skills, I was blabbing kind of a lot. Where one of the now roaming, chatting family members might overhear me—before we'd told Kim.

If Autumn was surprised (or impressed), she didn't show it. She just glanced back at the mausoleum. "Well, technically we didn't *bury* anybody. But I wouldn't put that kind of thing past a Mistmantle. You're sure?"

"Pretty sure," said Percy.

"He's pretty sure," I corrected. "I'm positive."

"So Kim is a Mistmantle." Autumn tapped the fingers of her right hand against her thumb, one by one, over and over. I'd seen her do the same thing at Holly Tree Lane; it seemed to be a thinking gesture. She was a fidgeter, like Percy. "Does she know?"

"Not yet," I said, "but she obviously has a right to. We're going to tell her today."

"Any chance you'll let me join you when you do?"

An odd request. I cocked my head at her. "Why?"

"I want to see her reaction. I asked her some questions about the spellbook, trying to subtly confirm it *was* a spellbook, and she was really cagey about it. I think she knows more than she's letting on."

I pointed at her. "Her mother was cagey about it, too."

"So the strategy is to gang up on her?" Percy clapped his hands, then rubbed them together. "Sign me up."

"Percy and Minerva!" Mrs. B called. She was heading toward us with Elaine, Phil, and a man I didn't recognize in tow. "*There* you are! We've been *looking* for you."

"See you later, then." Autumn gave us a little wave and walked away just as the others were upon us.

"Sorry we were late," I said to Mrs. B. "There was a whole thing with the florist. Actually, I really need to be getting back to Kim's."

"But John wanted to meet you!" said Mrs. B. "This is John Hollander. Kim's son."

John, huh? So she'd named him after her grandfather. I wondered whether that was her idea, or Barbara's. I hadn't met any of Kim's kids yet, although all three were supposed to be in attendance today. They'd done, as far as I could tell, absolutely nothing for this event.

John struck me as one of those men who was just short of handsome and charming enough to get away with things, but thought he was all the way there. He gave us an affable but slightly smarmy smile as he shook hands first with Percy, then with me. "I wanted to thank the person who planned all of this."

"Happy to do it," I lied.

Phil gave me a brotherly nudge. "Minerva can organize events in her sleep. She did an amazing job on our wedding."

I smiled my thanks. I liked Phil a lot, and not just because he was a fizzing vet to Plant. It was nice to have a fellow outsider to the utterly mad family that was the Bairds.

John flashed another broad smile. There was that wide mouth again, like Barbara's. And Lester Mistmantle's. "I heard you're also the bigshot detective around Bryd Hollow."

I blinked at him. "Where would you have heard such a thing?"

"From *me*, of course." Mrs. B put her arm around

my shoulders and gave me a squeeze. She sounded down-right proud, which was quite a turnaround from how furious she'd been when I interfered with her husband's murder investigation.

"They tell me you're looking into Edith's death," said John. "Not so much Gran's, though."

"No," I said, "not Barbara's, but our police chief is excellent at her job. She'll get to the bottom of it."

"Any idea who she's looking at?"

I shook my head. I did have some ideas, but none I was about to share with him. Especially since she'd told us Kim was still a suspect. I assumed Basil must be as well, and anybody else who'd come in contact with Edith's—Tilly's—things and was in a position to sell them. Although Basil wouldn't have tipped the police off about the watch sale if he were the one who'd arranged it. And then there was the nameless, faceless Tybryd employee everybody seemed to suspect. Notably, nobody on that list was an Eastern European woman.

Apparently John had some ideas of his own. "Well, if she's as smart as you say she is, she's got her eye on my mom."

Mrs. B gasped. I supported the sentiment. What a thing to say about his own mother. I bet Percy was loving it, though.

I decided a leading question was in order. "Kim would have no reason to steal things from her own mother, would she?"

John snorted. "My mother is not as smart as she thinks she is, but she's no fool either. She'd know enough to make it look like a theft. Without that, the only person with a motive is her."

"But what motive would she have?" I asked, in as innocent a voice as I could muster. "They seemed so close."

That earned me another snort. "You bought that?" John stuffed his hands into his pockets and shook his head, looking like a disappointed dad. "You're not living up to that detective reputation at *all*."

"What do you mean?" asked Percy.

"I'm the only one who was really close to Gran. She and Mom *despised* each other."

Chapter Thirteen

KIM'S HOUSE WAS BIG, expensive, and falling apart. We'd done a pretty good job of sprucing it up at Mrs. B's expense, but no amount of fancy floral arrangements and table linens could hide the water stains on the ceilings, or the dark, rotted bits on the hardwood floor near the back door. The crown molding in the living room was starting to separate from the wall. The furniture that was stretched out to cover all six thousand square feet had seen better days decades ago.

Percy and Autumn joined me in helping clean up after the reception—and we were the only ones. Even the kid who was staying with Kim (not John, he was in the poshest hotel he could find) left to go meet a friend, half an hour before the place cleared out. The fact that we were more considerate to the woman than her own children made me feel a lot better about having an ulterior motive for it.

While Autumn put leftovers into containers, Percy rinsed dishes for me to load into the dishwasher. Doing dishes was a skill he'd learned mostly at my apartment, since he did pretty much nothing for himself at home. Dante had also taught him to make scrambled eggs a couple of months before. Baby steps.

Kim's role in the cleaning process seemed to be mainly supervisory. She must have been willing to set aside her grudges if it meant she got some free labor, because she'd directed surprisingly few passive-aggressive accusations of murder at Percy.

He looked over at her as he handed me a plate. "So, I know this is probably an awkward time to bring this up, but we need to talk to you about your great-grandmother."

"Edith?"

"Turns out that wasn't her name."

That was my cue to step in and give a brief overview of the whole Edith-is-Tilly situation, but I was momentarily distracted by Tabitha. Barbara's—now Kim's, and sadly not Snick's—cat had spent the reception upstairs, sitting on a windowsill in a spare bedroom. Now she sauntered into the kitchen and came directly to the dishwasher to inspect our work. Apparently she wasn't impressed, because she gave me a very imperious look before jumping onto the breakfast table and curling up out of reach of Kim's shooing hand.

"You are the most annoying cat. I can't believe Mother let you just sit on any furniture you felt like." Kim transferred her scowl from Tabitha to Percy. "What are you talking about?"

I answered for him, starting with the fact that the real Edith Cotswold did not appear in any photographs from the year between *Titanic* and her disappearance, and ending with the fact that our skeleton lady—who was now, I guessed, an ash lady—had no biological relationship with Edith's surviving family. To supply the identity of the imposter, I filled in a little bit about Edith's lady's maid, and how we were pretty sure that was her family emblem on the medallion and the book. I did not mention witchcraft—yet.

Kim cast a couple of glances at Autumn while I spoke. As if checking for her reaction, even as Autumn was doing exactly that to Kim. Kim herself didn't look particularly shocked or appalled. When I finished she just said, "Okay."

"Okay?" I closed the dishwasher and turned around to lean my back against the counter, the better to study her expression. "You're not surprised?"

"I guess I am," she said with a shrug. "But it doesn't matter, right?"

I blinked at her. "Doesn't matter?"

"Edith might not have been my great-grandmother, but Roderick Baird was still my great-grandfather, right? It doesn't sound like anyone is denying that this woman —Trudy or whatever, the maid—had Roderick's baby." Kim tossed her head at Percy. "Since you're so into DNA tests, we could do one, if you need proof. I've seen pictures of Roddy, he looked just like my grandpa."

Of course her main concern was that nobody was questioning that she was a Baird. Being a Cotswold wasn't quite as much of a priority. "I agree, the resemblance was pretty strong," I said. "I don't think anybody is going to question John's paternity."

"But I will do a test, if it would ease your mind," Percy offered.

Kim waved that off. "My mind doesn't need easing. Unless anyone's trying to claim what little is left of my grandfather's estate."

Autumn slammed the refrigerator door and turned to lean against it, much like I'd just done with the counter—and with the same expression of bewildered irritation I'd probably been wearing at the time. She crossed her arms. "And that's it? That's all you have to say about this. You don't have a single question."

Kim looked at her like she'd just discovered a giant insect putting away her leftovers for her. "What would you like me to ask? I never knew my great-grandmother. And I obviously never knew the real Edith Baird, either. One stranger isn't much different from another. Or were you expecting me to freak out because she was a maid?"

Personally, I'd have been way more freaked out that she was a murderer and a hornswaggler, but to each their own, I guessed. Knowing Kim, she was at least a *little* freaked out about the maid thing—unless she'd already known all of this, and had her freakout long ago.

Kim narrowed her eyes, not at Autumn but at Percy. "Bet *you're* freaked out that a whole branch of your family came from a maid."

Percy laughed. "I don't have any need to be a snob."

He was maybe a hair more of a snob than he realized —he couldn't help it, honestly, none of them could— but for the most part, he was right. The Bairds were amazingly down to earth, for being some of the oldest money America had. And why shouldn't they be? The worst snobs were always the people who were almost rich, almost elite. People who'd just missed the mark by an inch or two. People like Kim.

People like Percy didn't need to jockey for position. Their position was assured. That wasn't a class I'd ever envisioned myself becoming part of—or raising a family in. But what could I say, the man made me laugh.

While I was contemplating grand issues of class dynamics and childrearing and the necessity of laughter in a longterm relationship, Kim was insisting that *she* didn't have any need to be a snob, either. "My great-grandmother's parentage has no bearing on me."

Or on her Baird genes, which was clearly the main thing.

"Maybe not," said Autumn, "but I would think it's had some bearing on you that she was a witch."

"A wi—what?" Kim burst out laughing, but it sounded forced.

Autumn snorted. "Please. You knew all along what was in that book. Probably recognized the focus for what it was, too."

Kim sniffed. "I have no idea what you're talking about."

"Of course you do."

"How does she?" I asked.

"And how do you know she does?" Percy added.

"Because." Autumn pointed at Tabitha, whose eyes were closed now. She didn't appear to have any interest in our conversation, or in us in general. "*That* is a familiar."

"Familiars are a thing?" I pushed away from the counter, moving closer to the breakfast table where

Tabitha lay. She looked like a regular cat. "Is that what Gravy is?"

"Depends on your definition, and more or less." Autumn hesitated, chewing at her lip. Maybe she was trying to decide how to explain. Or maybe just thinking about whether she wanted to. "Nature can be useful, sort of like a little boost to your power. Some witches imbue certain metals to make focuses, like Tilly's medallion. Some people have animal companions who help."

She looked back at Kim. "And that one there is yours."

Kim threw back her head and made a noise of long suffering, half groan, half sigh. "That is *not* my cat. And I'm not a witch."

"But your mother was?" I wasn't sure why I felt the need to ask. The woman had (apparently) owned a familiar.

"She *thought* she was." Kim shot Tabitha a glare, like the cat was the one interrogating her. "Fine. Yes, she thought she was a witch. I never went in for that mumbo-jumbo myself, but to each their own. She was into it."

"So the book and the medallion." Autumn's eyes lit. "They really are a real Mistmantle spellbook, and a real Mistmantle focus. After all these years." She shook her head, as if she couldn't quite believe it, even though we'd pretty much known that for a while. Still. It was good to have it confirmed.

And Kim had known all along that two of the items stolen from her mother were used for witchcraft, and hadn't said a thing. What else had she been keeping from us?

Possibly that she despised her mother?

Maybe Percy had been right to suspect her, after all.

I sat down at the breakfast table and scratched Tabitha behind the ear. Was it still okay to pet familiars, like they were regular pets? She started purring, so I guessed it was. I had a lot of questions about this familiar thing. Starting with why Autumn could recognize a familiar on sight, when she'd told us she couldn't identify witches. They seemed like similar skills. But I figured I'd save all that for later, in case she'd been bluffing.

"So," I said to Kim, "you knew your great-grandmother was a witch, and that she'd handed down a spellbook. Did you know she was really Tilly Mistmantle?"

Kim puffed out another irritated sigh. "No. How would I? I didn't know what that bear-leaf thing meant."

Let her be irritated. At least she was talking. Maybe she didn't want to make us mad, for fear we'd stick her with the balance on the catering bill. She was almost certainly still hoping to sell some things to Autumn. Looking around the house, I could see why she'd been acting so greedy. The woman was underwater, and possibly sinking fast. It seemed pretty common for posers like her to buy more house than they could afford, just to keep up an appearance, and then sit inside eating peanut butter and jelly to compensate.

"Do you think your mother knew?" I asked.

Kim's eyes flicked to the ceiling, like maybe she was praying for patience. "How? Her father never spoke to his mother. He found that book with whatever things of hers the aunt who raised him saved. He figured out what he could do with it—or thought he could—and passed that on to my mother."

"It's the family affinity," Autumn said with a nod. "He was a Mistmantle. Nobody had to teach him how to use Mistmantle spells. He just needed to do exactly what the book said, and they'd come out right. Like following a recipe."

Kim scoffed. "Whatever. You know, if we have to have a whole thing about the stupid witch stuff, you might as well make some coffee."

She was something, that Kim. But I got up to make coffee anyway, even though I didn't drink it. Which turned out to be a good thing, since all she had was instant.

"So your grandfather passed this on to his daughter, but she didn't pass it on to you?" I asked as I pulled mugs out of her cabinet.

"She tried." Kim looked away, picking at a placemat. "Whatever," she said again. "I don't believe in any of that junk."

"Don't believe it?" Autumn's voice was surprisingly gentle. "Or rejected it when you realized you can't do magic?"

"Hold on." While he spoke, Percy put one of the mugs back in the cabinet. No coffee for him. "I thought you just said Mistmantle spells worked for Mistmantles."

Autumn pulled a face at the tin of instant coffee. "None for me, thanks. Sure, but John was half a Mistmantle, which if my math is right made Barbara a quarter, and Kim here only an eighth."

"But John—your son, not your grandfather—is a witch," I said to Kim, putting two and two together. "He told us you hated your mother, and that he was the only one who was really close to her. Is this why? Because he's a witch and you're not?"

I had no idea how the genetics worked out on that one, unless John's father was also a witch. But then again, this whole witchcraft thing probably didn't have a firm basis in science. All it would take to cause a rift between Kim and John was for them to believe it.

Kim rolled her eyes. "Johnny's always had a flair for the dramatic. And he loves finding a sucker who'll indulge him."

"Okay." I decided that how much of a sucker I was or was not could be tabled for another time. "So why didn't you say anything, when the book and the focus were stolen?"

"What was I going to say?" Kim laughed. "That they were magical? Yeah, I'm sure that would've gone over great. It's irrelevant, anyway. People knew they found some valuable old things buried at Tybryd, and *someone*"—she gave Percy a pointed look that added the words *who works for you* for her—"decided they'd like to sell them before Mother could. End of story."

Percy threw his own look back at her. "If you say so."

She narrowed her eyes at him. "You know, she told you she brought the book to Tybryd to match it to Edith's necklace, but that's not really why."

"Okay, I'll bite." Percy crossed his arms. "What did she bring it for? To cast some spells?"

"To curse you."

"Me?" Percy's brows shot up. "Personally?"

"The Bairds. As a family. That's one of the reasons we were staying a week. The moon was going to be full on Tuesday."

"You were waiting for a full moon. Because the spell required it." Percy looked at Autumn, lips twitching. "That's a thing?"

"Sometimes. It goes back to that nature thing again. It's mostly only old spells that use events like that, though. We don't usually do spells that big anymore. They tend to get us in trouble." Autumn pursed her lips at Kim. "What kind of curse?"

"A curse of"—Kim made finger quotes—"'whispers.' That's what Mother called it, anyway."

I didn't love the mildly alarmed expression on Autumn Trelayne's face. "Is that bad?" I asked as I set Kim's coffee down in front of her. "If you want milk or sugar for that, you'll have to get it yourself."

Autumn grimaced, sucking air through her teeth. "It's killed more than a few of my folk over the centuries."

"What does it do?" I sat back down and resumed petting Tabitha, who still seemed to appreciate it. *You wouldn't have participated in putting an evil curse on anybody, would you?* I thought at her. If she answered me with her mind powers, I didn't hear it.

"Pretty much what it sounds like," said Autumn. "People will whisper about you. Rumors, gossip. Secrets. Eventually they'll start whispering about what should be done about the secrets, and the whispers turn to threats. Or worse. There've been whole"—she flung an arm—

"well, *witch hunts* that started with a curse of whispers. That whole thing in Salem?"

"*No.*" I gaped at her. "Salem, as in 1692 Salem?"

"Yep. It was only supposed to affect one family, but it got out of hand." Autumn sat down in the chair closest to me, but not before tossing a look over her shoulder at Percy. "*Probably* wouldn't have ended in the gallows for you, but it could've gotten bad, with a family like yours. Old, rich, sometimes in the public eye. Not immune to the occasional scandal."

"It was her revenge." Percy took the last seat at the table, his eyes fixed on Kim. He was actually mad, I realized, despite his breezy dismissal of all things witchcraft. He might not believe in curses, but apparently he found the idea of having one cast on him offensive nevertheless. "Against my family, for what they did to Edith. Tilly. For spreading rumors about her, saying she was a thief, and that she ran off."

"Instead of bothering to look for her." Kim's lazy tone made it clear she could not have been more bored with this conversation. "Plus all the slights that came after. You met my mother. You know how big that chip on her shoulder was."

"So she finally got her invitation to Tybryd," said Percy, "and that's what she decided to do with it. She couldn't have used a Georgia full moon?" He wiggled his fingers in what had become his official gesture for magic. "It had to be shining over Tybryd when the crow cawed at midnight?"

"Don't be silly, you wouldn't use *crows* in that ritual," Autumn said, with a not entirely straight face.

"They're so unreliable, you know? But she'd have needed personal items."

Kim snickered. "She took your forks. From lunch that day. Yours and your mother's."

"She took—" Percy sputtered. "How—what in the *actual h*—"

"Okay!" I jumped in. This seemed like a good time to herd us back toward a point. "So. We've confirmed that the spellbook is a spellbook—an active one, apparently—and the focus is a focus." I looked at Percy. "The only thing Mrs. Gochev tried to sell is the watch. Is that because she didn't know the other things were so valuable? Or because she *did* know and wanted to keep them?"

Percy spread his hands. "Or option three, she did sell them, and we just don't know it. She'd want to sell those to a witch, obviously."

"What's this about the watch?" Autumn asked.

I guessed Kim hadn't gotten around to telling her. Or to trying to sell it to her. She'd probably known from the start that Autumn was only interested in witchy things. I gave a brief summary of the botched sale in Asheville. Autumn's brow furrowed more and more as I spoke.

"So obviously the watch wasn't the motive for the murder," she said when I finished.

"How is that obvious?" asked Kim. "I still say if the watch was the only thing this Gochev woman—probably one of Tybryd's maids, by the way—tried to sell, it's the only thing she cared about."

I shook my head. Hearing my own summary, it had

become obvious to me as well. Especially immediately after hearing about the book being used for witchcraft right here in modern times, by modern witches. "Trying to dump the watch in a nearby city—a small city—so soon after the murder, to *somebody who knew Basil*, was sloppy." I pointed at Percy. "Didn't I say to you afterward that it was weird?"

"You did," he agreed. "And I said she probably just panicked. And probably had no idea the guy knew Basil."

"Which was sloppy of her," I said firmly. "Think about it. She didn't do the slightest bit of research before she picked somebody to contact? That dealer *golfs* with Basil. And since she was never sloppy up to that point, I don't think we can assume she was being sloppy with this."

Percy blinked at me. "You think she threw the sale on purpose?"

"More or less."

"*She* might not even be a she," said Autumn. "My guess is, the killer was afraid somebody would start asking questions about the focus, and maybe even the book."

"Somebody already *had* started asking questions," I interjected. "I was asking questions about that bear emblem from the second I saw it. You were asking questions. Maybe they even found out that Percy and I went to Poplar Knot. There don't seem to be so many thriving businesses there that they couldn't guess why."

"Actually, Poplar Knot is populated almost entirely by my folk." Autumn tipped her chin at Percy. "You were right: the killer *did* panic. So they made the crime all about the watch again, and set the police—and they hoped everyone else—on the trail of some middle-aged Bulgarian woman who was only after money." She raised her hands, like a magician showing there was nothing up her sleeves. "No witches to see here."

"They knew the sale would probably go wrong," I said. "Because they made sure to tip off somebody who would tip off the police for them. But you'll notice they also made sure 'Mrs. Gochev' didn't get caught. They *sacrificed* the watch, to use it as a decoy. Maybe they never even cared about it at all."

"Of course they cared about it!" Kim snapped. "It was the only thing that was worth anything. Nobody *killed* anyone over this other woo-woo nonsense."

But I had a feeling that woo-woo nonsense was exactly why Barbara had been killed.

Percy shifted in his chair, drumming his fingers against the table. He'd been arguing all along that the killer was only after money, that the watch was their main target. But now he didn't look quite so sure. "You said from the start that it was weird the killer took the book. I assumed they just took it because Barbara had it sitting with the other stuff."

"Except how would they know it was worth taking?" I asked. "Plenty of people knew about the things that were buried with Tilly, and those things had cachet, because of the story behind them. Even the wedding band was worth more than it was worth, if you know what I mean. But the book was just an old book."

"Unless they recognized the Mistmantle emblem," said Autumn, "and already knew it was worth taking."

I remembered Ruby's words: *murder is always either love or money.*

But maybe sometimes it was power.

Maybe the Mistmantle objects had been what the killer was really after all along—not because they wanted to sell them, but because they wanted to use them.

Autumn nodded at me. "We're looking for a witch."

Chapter Fourteen

AT LEAST SOMETHING good came of spending the better part of a day with Kim Hollander: on our way out I casually mentioned how much everybody at Baird House had loved having Tabitha there, and how very happy they would be if she went to live there permanently. And that would, after all, be keeping her in the family, wouldn't it? Kim took Snick's number.

While Percy drove Mrs. B and Elaine to the airport the next morning, I met Autumn Trelayne for breakfast at a diner the size of a railroad car. We had some things to discuss.

I'd expected Percy to fight me on it, like he always did, raising trivial arguments like *it's dangerous* and *you'll get yourself killed* and *how many times have you been shot already*. But he'd just shaken his head, told me he hoped the french toast was good, and kissed me goodbye. Maybe he'd finally learned his lesson, as far as telling me what he thought I should and should not be doing was concerned. Or maybe he just thought a literal witch hunt was such an insane idea that there was no danger of it actually working.

Autumn had distinctly said that *we* were looking for a witch. She was obviously invested enough in trying to find the Mistmantle focus and spellbook to dig into Barbara's murder. As for me, I hadn't solved Tilly's murder, and wasn't sure if I could. But Tilly's murder had led to her granddaughter's. Maybe I could at least help with that. Besides, I had never let a little thing like it being none of my business stop me from investigating a murder before. I saw no reason to start now.

Because really, if not us, then who? Everybody else was looking for a stout, greedy Eastern European woman. Even after our conversation yesterday, Kim (and to a lesser extent Percy) wasn't convinced that a witch had killed Barbara Hingley solely to claim two powerful artifacts that the witches thought had been lost over a century ago. I could only imagine the look Ruby Walker would give me, if I told her the same thing. Her glasses might spontaneously combust.

But I was convinced. It wasn't the *only* explanation that fit the evidence I had; it still could've been a non-witch who knew enough about witches to recognize the Mistmantle emblem and know they could sell Tilly's things for a lot of money. But that seemed a lot less likely than a witch making that connection. It didn't matter whether I was (or wasn't) as skeptical of witchcraft as Percy was, or as Kim claimed to be. It didn't matter whether I believed the Mistmantle objects contained any actual power. All that mattered was that, if Autumn was any indication, the people who called themselves witches *did* believe it.

I could, of course, produce no proof whatsoever to support this theory. Hence the breakfast. If we were right that we were looking for a witch, we needed a plan to find them.

Them as in *him*, *her*, or singular or plural *them*: it could have been any of those. Given that "Mrs. Gochev" was probably a decoy, it seemed safe to assume she was either somebody in disguise, or another intermediary, like Carl. Or at least not working alone. Either way, the killer still could have been anybody.

"So," I said, as soon as our server took our orders and walked out of earshot, "Percy still thinks it's Kim. He thinks the whole thing about panicking and dumping the watch supports that, because that happened after you started asking her about her mother's things. Plus it got her the watch back so she could sell it legitimately."

"Hmph," Autumn drummed her fingers against the table. "Do *you* think it's Kim?"

I shrugged. I didn't, and never really had, but that was just my hunch. "She's definitely a suspect. I might not be surprised to find out she was involved. But if she did do it, I imagine it would've been to sell the other things too—to a witch. Which means there's also a witch involved. Unless you're wrong about her not having power herself."

"I don't think I'm wrong about it," said Autumn. "Her mother's familiar doesn't like her *at all*. Good thing you might have gotten the poor girl out of there. She needs a proper retirement."

I leaned forward, hands wrapped around my warm mug. "How do you know she doesn't like her? Can you talk to them telepathically?" If she said yes, I would think she was raving mad, obviously. And not be at all jealous.

But she only laughed. "Probably no better than you can. You don't know what Plant's thinking?"

"Plant has a very expressive face. And a very judgy one."

"So do most cats."

"Fair point."

Autumn gestured to the server for more coffee. She'd already finished her first cup, before my tea was even what I considered properly cooled off. "I think we're more in tune with our familiars than most strangers are with their pets. But I'd say we communicate in pretty much the ordinary ways."

Huh. Witchcraft turned out to be kind of boring. What was the point in magic, if you couldn't even use it to talk to your pets? "Well, that's a shame. If you could talk to Tabitha, she could probably tell us who killed Barbara. We need to be looking further than Kim. If she wasn't involved—and possibly even if she was—somewhere in Bryd Hollow is a witch who got a good enough look at the focus at least, if not the book, to recognize the Mistmantle emblem."

Autumn nodded. "The focus was probably motive enough. They might not even have known about the book until they saw it."

"All right, so that's ..." I counted them out from the

beginning. "The tree guy. Pretty much the entire police force, I'm sure. The medical examiner. Me, Percy, Mrs. B, probably Elaine, she drops by the house a lot. But I'm comfortable that I didn't murder Barbara without my knowledge, and I'll vouch for the Bairds, too. Everybody I asked about the bear symbol. Everybody who ate lunch the day Barbara and Kim arrived. Everybody who works at Baird House, probably, including the day maids. Ned —a kid who works for me—came and got Tabitha, and I think the stuff was out on the table while he was there. And Basil and Lilian—she's the art director at Tybryd— both took some pictures. So anybody they showed those to after lunch that day, but before Barbara was murdered that night."

"That's a pretty big suspect pool." Autumn fidgeted with her fork. "I don't suppose you know which of them might be witches?"

"No. Some of them I only really know by name. And I don't even know that, for some of the others. *Anybody Basil talked to* isn't exactly a full name and address, is it? But I have an idea for how to narrow down the witch part."

The server came with my french toast and Autumn's omelet, and I paused while we started on our food. Hers looked so good, I kind of wished she were Percy, so we could swap plates halfway through. "It might sound a little bit far-fetched, though."

Autumn snorted around her mouthful of bacon. "Your boyfriend thinks I live way out in Narnia, and you're worried *I'll* think *your* ideas are far-fetched?"

My face heated. "I'm sorry about him. He doesn't do it to be mean."

She looked a little taken aback. "I don't think he was ever *mean*. I don't mind a little teasing. I like funny people."

"You think he's funny?"

"Don't you?"

I took a sip of tea to hide what I was sure was a sappy smile. "Yeah, I do. But don't tell him that, he's already convinced he's the most hilarious person on the planet. Cracking jokes is his answer to everything. It's how he copes with the world."

"You should hang on to him, then. Being able to make light of any situation, up to and including murder, is an important quality in a life partner. If you ask me."

I hadn't asked her, of course, but I didn't mind the advice. I'd been thinking much the same thing yesterday, about Percy making me laugh. And even though she seemed a little younger than I was, I had the sense Autumn Trelayne was an old soul. "Thank you, I intend to hang on to him."

She gave me an impish smile. "I suppose it doesn't hurt that he's so rich."

I dragged my fork through the syrup on my plate, avoiding her eye. I had friends in Bryd Hollow, obviously, but they were Percy's friends, too. I didn't discuss our relationship with them. And my sister was rarely any help; she'd started shrieking for me to marry him the second she heard the word *Baird*. "It doesn't help as much as you'd think," I admitted. "We come from pretty different worlds."

Autumn dismissed that with a wave and a hearty *Psssh*. "So what, you're both in Bryd Hollow now, and that strikes me as a pretty small world."

I hadn't thought of it that way. "Very true. I guess the question is whether it's a world with witches in it."

She leaned forward, ready to get down to business. "So what's your plan?"

"Well, Ivy can identify witches, right?" That was what she'd said back at Holly Tree Lane, and I—bizarrely maybe, all things considered—was willing to trust her on that. It needn't be mind reading or magic, this knack Ivy had. Maybe she could tell by body language, or a look in their eye, or the way they carried themselves. Maybe there was some pattern to their behavior that the rest of us couldn't see. Maybe she was just unusually perceptive. Some dogs were like that; I didn't see why people couldn't be like that, too.

"Yyyyes ..." Autumn said, "but I don't think we can bring Ivy door to door and demand people submit to her inspection. There's probably a rule."

I stopped myself from rolling my eyes at her. Maybe she wasn't offended by Percy because she *was* Percy. "But what if I had a short list of people ready in advance? We could probably arrange to run into them."

"And how are you going to come up with this short list?"

"That's the far-fetched part. I've only ever heard of one instance of supposed witchcraft in Bryd Hollow. A curse, back in the early 1900s somewhere."

"So somewhere in the same decade when Tilly was killed, there were witches in Bryd Hollow?"

"I thought of that too. I don't know of Molly Towe having anything to do with the Bairds, but I don't know much about her at all. This curse was another family she was mad at." I waved my fork before taking another bite of french toast. "It's a long story, there was this whole thing with a knife, and somebody's fiancé, and Henry VIII."

Autumn's brows shot up. "Did you just say Henry VIII?"

"Yeah." I inhaled sharply and lowered my voice. "Why, was he a witch?"

"Not that I ever heard. Supposedly a couple of his wives were."

"Yeah, I'll bet I can guess which ones." But I didn't. If I got on the Tudor train, I might not get off for hours, and Autumn was almost done with her eggs. I forced myself back to the subject at hand. "Anyway, Bryd Hollow has a lot of longstanding families in it. And like any small town, it tends to have a lot of lifers. If I did a little research, I could probably find a fair number of people still living there who are related to Molly Towe."

"And then cross reference that list with the people who might have seen the focus." Autumn sat back and took a long sip from her third cup of coffee. "That would certainly be a place to start, anyway."

"I thought so, too. Do you think Ivy would be willing to come to Bryd Hollow to help us?"

"Oh, for *sure*," Autumn said, adding a vigorous nod for good measure. "Holly and Ivy will both want to come. Their lives aren't all that exciting. Our lives. But at least I get out of Poplar Knot in search of heirloom spell-books, now and then."

First they couldn't talk to their pets, now they had uneventful lives? Witchcraft really was boring.

"Well then," I said. "Sounds like we have a plan."

IT WAS during phase one of this plan that I was once again distracted by Tilly's case. I was up late the night after we got back from Georgia, Plant on my lap and my laptop on Plant, tracing the progeny and the progeny's progeny of one Molly Towe of Bryd Hollow, North Carolina. Make that *very* late; I'd long since finished my pile of taffy when my computer announced the arrival of an email from Jane-Ann Weaver, which meant it was already morning her time.

She'd gotten my message about the DNA results, she said, but it was the *strangest thing*. (Even though Jane-Ann was only in her thirties, in my head she sounded like Mrs. B with an English accent.) She'd called her cousin Lizzie to tell her the news. Fourth cousin, but they'd gotten in touch over this whole thing, if I could believe it, and gotten friendly. Lizzie had been *dying* to hear how it turned out.

Lizzie's mother was Julia Seaton (but not *the* Julia Seaton, Jane-Ann assured me, whoever that was), and Julia's mother was Pauline Dixon, née Cotswold, who was the granddaughter of Harry Cotswold, Edith's brother. It took me a minute, probably owing to the late hour, to follow all of that, but I got it eventually.

And Julia had told Lizzie, who'd called Jane-Ann back to tell her, that the whole thing was a big mistake. The Edith who came to America aboard the *Titanic* and then the *Carpathia* had definitely been the real Edith.

Her proof: Harry had visited Edith and her new family in America.

I didn't need to write back to ask whether Lizzie and her mother were sure of this, because Jane-Ann had already asked them for me. They were sure, because Pauline Cotswold Dixon—who was now ninety-three years old, if I could believe it, but still sharp as anything —was sure. Not only was that her grandfather's first trip to America, but he hit it off with the Bairds while he was there. He ended up investing in one of the Baird family ventures, a risky scheme that paid off. Harry's branch of the Cotswold family was to this *very day* much more well off than the other Cotswolds, not that Jane-Ann minded, because they were *lovely*, and it was all down to Edith's good marriage and that trip. That was where their fortune was made.

A family legend of sorts, I guessed, like Edith's romantic goodbye to her new husband on the deck of the *Titanic*. And her presence at the 1913 house party. She seemed to be the center of a lot of stories. She'd had quite a life—most of it after she died.

Jane-Ann was sure I could see as well as she could that the DNA test must have been wrong, and that Edith *must* have been Edith. Harry would have known if his sister wasn't really his sister.

On that last point, we agreed. Where we differed was on what he must have done with that knowledge.

Jane-Ann—and Lizzie, Julia, and Pauline—believed Harry's story, which he'd probably relayed to his children much as they'd passed it down, finally, to me. And who knows, there might have been some truth to it. He might really have seeded his fortune on that trip.

By investing what he'd made from blackmailing Tilly Mistmantle.

Chapter Fifteen

I EMAILED JANE-ANN BACK, asking if there was any way she or Lizzie could find out the approximate dates of Harry's visit, just the season and the year would do. Obviously it was somewhere between May of 1912 and midsummer 1913—but exactly where in that span was crucial. I also asked if they might have any photographs from that visit, or photographs of him at all. I had no doubt that I would never find Harry Cotswold's face in a Baird photo as a family chum (or hopeful friend). But I would have to comb back through Emily's journal entries from the days around midsummer, and see if I could find anything that might be descriptive of Tilly's mysterious visitor.

In the meanwhile, I had more modern priorities. I'd found a few candidates for our Bryd Hollow witch among the Towe descendants I'd been able to trace, but one in particular stood out so much I practically tripped over her name when I saw it. Erin Radcliffe, Basil's wife, was Molly Towe's great-granddaughter.

She'd been at lunch with Basil that day; she'd gotten a close-up look at both the medallion and the book. Somewhere in the small talk, she must have heard where Barbara and Kim were staying, and that they were in two rooms rather than one. She knew she could catch Barbara alone.

Plus, she hated animals, which if you asked me was usually at least a little bit suspect. I guessed she wasn't the kind of witch who kept a familiar. Maybe that meant she'd needed a focus.

We were definitely going to start with Erin. And I had a strong feeling we were going to end there, too.

The Bryd Hollow Small Business Association was meeting the following Wednesday; I knew their schedule from prior attendance when I was an event planner. And I knew Basil would definitely be there—which meant that Erin would be at Yore on her own. And if I recalled correctly, Holly Tree Lane was closed on Wednesdays.

Autumn, Ivy, and Holly all agreed to come. In fact, Autumn decided to make a little trip out of it, and reserved a room at Tybryd for the night. (I offered to pay for that, but was refused.) None of them had ever been there, she said, and her cousins loved a road trip. She was even bringing Gravy along. He could hang out with Plant at Tailbryd while we were occupied in animal haters' places of business.

One person who would not be joining us: Percy. "I can't come to your thing," he informed me the weekend before, while we were having dinner at Deirdre's diner. "Your little sting operation. I'm sorry."

"Why not?" I asked, fully expecting the answer to be *Because I have less than no desire to.*

"I have to go to Chicago next week. I won't be back until Friday."

I frowned. "For the soap people?"

"Yeah."

"I thought Elaine was going to that."

"She was, but Phil has his vet banquet thing, and they just found out he's getting an award, so she wants to be there for him."

"So this is entirely about doing a favor for Elaine and not at all because you desperately do not want to be there."

"Of course I want to be there!"

I pointed my fork at him (after clearing it of meatloaf first). "You think my 'little sting operation' is vazey, and you just don't want to admit it."

"Don't be ridiculous. I have zero problem admitting I think it's vazey. Assuming vazey means stupid."

"More or less." Victorian slang had been a sort of code language between me and my sister as kids; it had started as a secret way to curse in front of a curse-intolerant father, and blossomed from there. I'd never shaken the habit, but Percy still didn't have it all quite down.

"Well then, it's vazey," he said. "At best, you'll embarrass yourself—"

"Embarrass myself?" I cut in. "Or embarrass you?"

"When have I ever cared about you embarrassing me? Wait." He held up his hands before I could close my gaping mouth and come up with a retort. "That came out wrong. You know what I mean. I've never *worried* about you embarrassing me. Because I've never had to. Because you're so wonderful and charming and all the good adjectives that will get me out of trouble right now."

"Because you do such a fine job of embarrassing yourself."

"Fine, then take it from an expert. You'll embarrass *yourself* at best. At worst, you'll end up confronting an unstable psycho who killed an old lady because they thought she had a magic necklace."

"Aren't all psychos unstable? Isn't that one of the pillars of psycho culture?"

"Thought she had a magic necklace," Percy repeated, clearly feeling I'd missed the point. "This is not your garden-variety psycho we're talking about."

I arched a brow. "And you hate to miss all that nanty-narking?"

He shrugged as he took a swig of his beer. "If you're there I'm there, right? But I'm assuming Autumn won't want to reschedule, now that they booked a room and everything."

Poor guy. Behind all the jokes, there really was an ocean of worry. I reached over to take his hand. "I know you want to protect me, but I'm covered. My team will have *way* more witches than the psycho team." I cocked my head, not having previously considered that an entire coven might have killed Barbara. "Probably."

Percy lifted my hand to his lips and kissed it, for once not laughing at a stupid joke. "Just ... don't get shot while I'm gone, yeah?"

I rolled my eyes. "I am not going to embarrass myself,

I am not going to put myself in a dangerous situation, and I am definitely not going to get shot."

Well. One out of three wasn't bad.

I WASN'T sure exactly what we'd do, if Ivy confirmed that Erin was a witch. Or for that matter, that any other resident of Bryd Hollow was a witch. I'd have to assess the situation first, and make a judgment call on whether I trusted Ivy's witch detector, and whether I thought whoever it was could really have killed Barbara.

But I supposed I would have to do that quickly, because if I did think we'd found the murderer, I should probably confront them right then and there, with the element of surprise on my side. I couldn't exactly take it to Ruby otherwise. *Erin Radcliffe is a not-garden-variety-psycho witch who hates animals and killed Barbara Hingley because she thought she had a magic necklace?* Yeah, I was pretty sure that wasn't going to fly. And I couldn't think of a better way to get proof of witchcraft than to get the witch to confess, or to at least say something incriminating enough to convince Ruby to pursue that line of investigation.

On the other hand, I'd promised Percy I wouldn't put myself in a dangerous situation. Did confronting a not-garden-variety-psycho witch count as dangerous, if I made sure to do it in a public place, with three other witches at my side?

It was an important question, one I put to Autumn Trelayne when she came to Tailbryd to drop off Gravy late Wednesday morning. The BHSBA meeting was a lunch this time around, so we didn't have long to bide our time. I'd had some champagne and Tybryd signature chocolates sent to Autumn's room; I hoped Holly and Ivy were sticking with the latter and saving the former for later.

If we'd caught a murderer by then, I would even join them.

"I told you before, magic requires spells," Autumn assured me, while I entered Gravy's information into the computer before sending him out to the now repaired Yard C to play with Plant. "Spells take preparation and time. She can't just flick her wrist and turn you into a newt. Especially not in the middle of her public store. You'll be fine."

I paused at my keyboard. "Do you think that's why Tilly didn't kill Harry Cotswold, instead of the other way around? I've been wondering that, how a guy gets the upper hand on a witch." Or I would have wondered that, if I believed in witchcraft, which I reminded myself I didn't ... really. Lately my thinking on the subject seemed to be getting a little muddy.

Autumn shrugged. "Witches' heads bash in as easily as any other head."

I thought of Barbara and grimaced. "Well, that's all well and good for protecting us from newt transformations, but suppose Basil and Erin keep a good old-fashioned gun behind their counter? They've got some pretty valuable stuff in Yore, it wouldn't be all that surprising if they did. I assume witches' heads are also as vulnerable to bullets as any other head?"

"Yes. But." Autumn rummaged through her purse. "Ivy made us these." Her hand finally emerged with what looked like a tiny straw doll on a black leather cord. "Protective charm. You wear it around your neck. Besides, there's still that whole public store thing. Erin's not just going to shoot three unarmed people in broad daylight in the middle of town."

It was a fair point. And I did put my charm on, although more out of politeness than anything. (Tucked under my shirt, where it couldn't be seen; whatever other virtues it may or may not have had, it wasn't much of a fashion statement.) But I was still nervous as we walked through the door at Yore.

The four of us together must have been quite a sight. Holly had swapped her pink hair for bright blue with green tips, and was wearing what looked like an oversized second-grader's outfit (if the second-grader had been allowed to dress themselves): wool tights in a pink and purple polka-dot pattern, with a blue and purple argyle sweater dress. Ivy, on the other hand, must have decided Tybryd called for fancy, and was wearing a long dress with high-heeled boots and pearls. Autumn and I looked underdressed in comparison, in plain jeans and long-sleeved t-shirts. March had just arrived, and spring with it. I hoped for the twins' sake that Erin was our culprit; they'd both get hot if we had to do much more walking around town.

Yore was a lovely shop, if a bit chaotic, crammed with furniture and clocks and jewelry. The smell of old things calmed me down a little, as it often did. As I'd expected, Erin was behind the counter. She greeted us with a closed-mouth smile, by way of multitasking and pursing her lips at Holly at the same time.

I asked if Basil was in, and was relieved when she told me he was at the meeting. At least things were going to plan. I put on a disappointed face. "What a shame, my friends are in town, and they're antique dealers, too."

Autumn stepped in on cue. "We deal mostly in books. I was hoping to take a look at some of yours, and ..."

In case it took Ivy a while to get a sense of Erin, we had a whole thing planned, wherein Autumn would offer to buy some of the few books Yore had. She'd suggest she would have an easier time moving them than Basil, and they'd dicker a little bit over price or something.

But none of that proved necessary. Ivy interrupted her cousin by leaning over the counter, studying Erin over the top of her glasses like she was preparing for the role of Ruby Walker in a play, and blurting, "She is *definitely* a witch. And she's powerful."

She gave first Autumn, then me a vigorous nod before turning to Erin to do the exact same nod a third time. "You're powerful."

Erin blinked at her. "I beg your pardon, did you just call me a witch?" Her own glasses were hanging from a chain around her neck. She put them on and studied Ivy in return, before shifting her gaze to me. "Who *are* these people?"

"Well, they're ... you don't recognize them?"

Erin cast another judgy glance at Holly. "I'm fairly certain I've never met them."

"No, I meant more along the lines of recognizing them as ... kindred spirits."

I was doing my best, but there was no way to ease into this, was there? As far as I knew, being a witch was a binary condition; you either were or you weren't. If Erin was going the route of pretending not to be, there was no middle ground to meet her in.

Holly elbowed her sister. "I don't think you were supposed to just toss it out like that, Ive. I figured we'd have a little chat and then go, and you would tell us afterward. Maybe regroup over lunch, figure out how to get proof of the murder."

Erin huffed. "Excuse me, the *murder*?"

"Ooh, lunch is a great idea!" said Ivy. "I'm starving. I told you we should've stopped on the road." She turned to me. "We're saving those chocolates you gave us for later. Thank you, by the way."

While she was smiling at me, Erin was gaping and glaring, and Autumn and Holly were giving me expectant looks, waiting for me to make a call on where to go from here. Which was fair, considering this was my mission.

Odsbodikins.

I was supposed to be confronting the witch, throwing her off balance so she would say or do something incriminating. Instead I was the one off balance. It was time to take this situation in hand, and turn it around.

"Erin," I said levelly, "we have reason to believe that you're a practicing witch, and that you murdered Barbara Hingley."

Erin's eyes flashed with anger. Because we'd just accused her of killing Barbara (and being a witch), and the idea was outrageous and offensive? Or because we'd just accused her of killing Barbara (and being a witch), and she was upset she'd been found out?

It was hard to say. Without another word, she marched past us, toward the door.

"You can't just let her leave!" Holly squealed.

But what were we supposed to do? Place her under citizen's arrest, on the grounds that Ivy Trelayne said she was powerful?

"Leave?" Erin scoffed. "Leave you four alone in here? As if. I'm just closing the store, so we can speak in private."

Was that better? I wasn't sure that was better. Getting locked in here with her didn't feel like strict adherence to my promise to Percy.

Erin had taken a set of keys out of the pocket of her long sweater, but she must have been nervous, because she dropped them before she could get the key in the door.

I rushed to speak while she was picking them up. "You don't need to do that! Maybe just turn the sign to *Closed*? I don't think any of us wants to be locked in here together. Including you, right?"

Her back was to me, so I couldn't see her face. But she must have taken my suggestion favorably, because when she straightened up, she put her keys back in her pocket, and turned the sign. Then she went back behind the counter. I supposed she liked having it between her and us, but I'd have preferred her hands where I could see them.

"Would you mind putting your hands on the counter while we talk?" I asked.

I fully expected her to tell me exactly where to go with that request, but she just folded her arms across her chest. "So," she said, "you've decided I killed Barbara."

I tried to keep my face and voice as neutral and unreadable as hers. "We have reason to suspect you. That's why we came. To clear it up."

"And you think witches kill people and steal their antique watches just because they're evil?" Erin gestured broadly around. "Maybe these are all things Basil and I stole from people we killed, huh?"

"*We're* witches," said Autumn. "We know they're not evil. And we know the watch isn't what you were after, so you can let that one go."

"I assume you recognized the Mistmantle emblem on the focus and the book, and that's why you took them?" I asked. I wasn't foolish enough to expect her to say *Why yes I did, and then I killed Barbara*. But maybe we could get her to let something slip.

Erin rolled her eyes. "The book. I didn't need the *book*."

"So you only wanted the focus?" Autumn looked confused.

I felt much the same. If she didn't need the book, why had she taken it? Well, to sell, I supposed. You wouldn't just leave it there. If you were going to go as far as murder, you might as well take everything.

Erin hesitated, then tossed her hands, as if giving up.

"You aren't very *smart* witches, are you? I was after the amulet!"

"The necklace," I said. Obviously that must be what she meant, but I had yet to hear it referred to as an amulet.

"Yes! It's the amulet of stars!"

Autumn crossed her arms. "The what now?"

"For breaking the curse," said Erin. "Don't tell me you didn't recognize it."

Curse? Now there was a curse? Did she mean the one Barbara had been planning? "What curse are we talking about?" I asked.

"The Curse of Never Existed," Autumn said. "She's stalling us."

By the time she got to the word *stalling*, the statement was unnecessary. The bell above the door chimed. I looked over my shoulder to find Ruby walking in, hands already on her hips.

"What in the devil is going *on* here?"

Chapter Sixteen

I KNEW we hadn't broken any laws. We hadn't threatened Erin. We'd even specifically asked her not to lock the door. And there was no way accusing a woman of witchcraft and murder one little time constituted harassment. I'd been called a witch (sometimes *with a B*, as it were) plenty of times by plenty of people, and Ruby hadn't arrested any of them.

But I didn't like being on Ruby's bad side. Or her worse side, anyway; I practically lived on the bad one. So I led my gang of errant witches over to the police station (which was a very short walk from Yore) and obeyed her request that we sit and wait in one of the interview rooms.

Then she went to talk to Erin. I could only imagine how that conversation was going. Or really, I couldn't. I was torn between calling myself a complete idiot for trusting Ivy, and wondering whether there was a spell for bewitching the police chief that Erin might, at that very moment, be casting.

Whether she was a normal person or just acting like one, Erin had done what any normal person would do, upon being cornered by four lunatics who seemed to want to hang her for a witch: created a distraction, then texted Ruby while she was bent over with her back to us, picking up her keys. She didn't pull the phone all the way out of her sweater pocket, lest we see it, and she had to be quick, so she only got out the numerals *9* and *1*.

Apparently that was enough. It turned out she and Ruby were friends.

We weren't waiting long before Ruby came in, closed the door, and immediately snapped at me.

"Why didn't you tell me this was witch business?"

"I ... what?" Of all the things I wasn't expecting her to say—ever—that had to be at the top of the list.

There was an empty seat at the table, but Ruby didn't sit. Instead she leaned against the wall, where she could look at us all from over the top of her glasses. To my surprise, her eyes finally came to rest not on me, but on Autumn. "So. You're the Trelaynes."

"Some of them," Autumn agreed.

"Wait, you know them?" I asked.

"I know of them. They've got a reputation among the witches up and down these mountains." Ruby tipped her chin at Autumn. "My Great-Aunt Silvie lived up in Boone. She was good friends with a June Trelayne."

"Oh!" Autumn looked at Ivy. "June was Grandad's cousin?"

"Grandad's aunt, I think," said Ivy.

For possibly the first time ever, I did not care to

examine the older branches of a family tree. I was too busy gaping at Ruby. "You are not a witch!"

I simply could not process any world in which Ruby Walker was anything but the stern, disapproving schoolmarm of a policewoman I knew her to be. The magical and the supernatural definitely did not line up with my view of her.

Besides, surely my friend Carrie would have told me if she and her Aunt Ruby were *witches*. Wouldn't she?

Maybe not. Autumn had said they didn't talk about it with non-witches much. And judging by Percy's reaction to the Trelaynes, Carrie would have good reason to keep quiet about it. She was the head of HR at Tybryd, and Percy was her boss as well as her friend. She wouldn't want him deciding she was a crackpot.

Thankfully, my worldview did not require so major an adjustment. Ivy shook her head before Ruby could answer. "No, she doesn't have the craft."

Ruby snorted. "No I do not, and thank goodness for that."

"But you're a believer?" I was still staring. Honestly, Ruby believing in witches was almost as surprising as if she were one herself. And to be such a big believer that she knew things about witches, well enough to know about the Trelaynes? Yet not well enough to recognize a focus or the Mistmantle family emblem.

"Silvie was my aunt by marriage," she said, "so I don't have the gene. Assuming it's a gene. And before you ask, no, Carrie never met her. But Silvie and I were close. Enough that she didn't feel a need to be careful around me. So yes, I believed what I saw with my own eyes, when it was put there by a person I trusted. What fool doesn't?"

That explained it, then. She knew North Carolina witch stuff thanks to a North Carolina witch. But she wasn't so steeped in witch culture that she'd known about the Mistmantles. "Fair enough," I said.

"Your approval is a great relief." Ruby took off her glasses and rubbed the bridge of her nose. "So. Ladies. My very confused friend Erin tells me you accused her of killing Barbara in order to get her hands on a book and a hocus. What's a hocus? That's a new one for me. Does it come with a pocus?"

"Not hocus, *focus*," I said. "We meant the necklace. And *somebody* killed Barbara to get it."

"Then I guess it's safe to assume this *Titanic* maid of yours is the witch who started all this way back when." She gave me a hard look. "So why didn't you tell me before?"

I tossed my hands, thinking the answer frankly too obvious to bother with. "Because I assumed you'd call me insane, like any normal person would do."

The glasses came back on. "If you had talked to me about it, I could've told you you're barking up the wrong tree. I don't think you'll find many witches in Bryd Hollow. And you're certainly not going to find any at Yore."

Ivy shook her head, her expression turning mutinous. "I am never wrong about a witch. Especially not when it's that strong. That woman has a lot of power."

Ruby spread her hands. "Maybe she does. But if so, she doesn't know it."

That was a third possibility I hadn't yet given much thought to, between Ivy being wrong, and Erin being a liar. I looked at Autumn. "Can that happen? Can you be a witch, or have witchy potential or whatever, without realizing it?"

"*I've* never seen it before," Ivy said. She looked down at the table, fidgeting with her fingers. "But then, I'm not exactly a globe trotter, am I?"

"Of course it's *possible*," said Autumn. "Maybe not *probable* in this case, when you consider a Bryd Hollow witch almost certainly killed Barbara, and Ruby just told us there aren't many witches here. What are the chances Erin Radcliffe is just a coincidence? But *possible*?" She waved a hand. "Sure. Witches joining stranger society, never teaching the craft to their children. Some people opt out, you know. It's a weird life. Not to mention all the persecution and burnings and whatnot. I mean, there's a whole cliché named after hunting us. Not everybody wants that."

I thought of Tilly, and all the trouble she'd gone through to steal a new life and leave the name Mistmantle behind. Roderick Baird hadn't been a witch. Maybe "opting out" was why she'd run away. But then, I supposed if that were the case, she wouldn't have kept using witchcraft. She'd been wearing her focus when she died. I doubted that was for sentimental value.

"And there must be orphans sometimes, like John Baird," I said. "What if he'd never found his mother's book and decided to give the spells a whirl? He never would've had any idea he had power. But somebody like Ivy still would've been able to sense it. Or so it would seem." I glanced at Ruby. "If you're right, that is, and Erin really isn't a witch."

"She really isn't a witch."

"With respect," I began, but Ruby rolled her eyes and interrupted before I could go on.

"Why is it that whenever you start a sentence with those two words, I know you're about to very *dis*respect-fully question my competence?"

"I'm not questioning your competence at all!" I protested. "I know how good at your job you are. But Erin is your friend, so you're bound to have a little unavoidable bias. And Autumn says they don't always tell their friends. Plus, this is a little outside your scope, isn't it? *Respectfully*, I'm not sure being Great-Aunt Silvie's great-niece really qualifies you as more of a witch authority than the Trelayne witches we've got sitting right here."

"Ah," Ruby said with a snort. "So you're not questioning my competence, only my qualifications."

"I'm only suggesting we *consider*—"

She held up a hand. "And I have. Weeks ago, as a matter of fact. Witch authority or not, good old-fashioned police work does qualify me to tell you that Erin did not kill Barbara. And neither did Basil, by the way, if you're interested. They have an alibi. They were at the high school when the crime was committed."

Odsbodikins, *Camelot*. I'd completely forgotten. But now that Ruby said it, I remembered them talking about it with Ned, that day at lunch. Basil's nephew or something was playing Sir Dinadan. Or Sir Lionel. One of the sirs who fails to kill Lancelot, anyway.

"And yes, I have confirmed that they were really there." Ruby gave me the glasses of doom one final time, as if I'd actually been fool enough to ask that question. "What exactly do you think I do here all day?"

Chapter Seventeen

I ASSUMED TERRORIZING AN APPARENTLY innocent woman and being dragged into the police station for a signature Ruby Walker Scolding was probably enough Bryd Hollow tourism for the Trelaynes. But I'd underestimated just how badly Autumn still wanted to find Tilly's things. She and her cousins wanted to check out the next closest of Molly Towe's descendants. Unlike Erin, none of the others on my list came from a direct line, but they splintered off in various straight and not-so-straight paths from Molly's siblings' branches of the Digby family tree.

So we went to the dry cleaner's (he was married to a police officer), the public library (where I'd inquired about the emblem), and a hospital half an hour away, where we pretended to be visiting a patient so we could sneak a look at one of the doctors (Lilian Berk's best friend). We even dropped by Rapunzel's restaurant for a peek at my old arch-nemesis Bonnie Digby, on the pretense of inquiring after reservations for that evening.

(There weren't any, as I knew there wouldn't be. Rapunzel's had a celebrity chef, and even in March they were almost always full.) I really couldn't see Bonnie as our killer, but I'll admit I wouldn't have minded being wrong.

I wasn't wrong. Neither Bonnie nor any of the others were witches. By Ivy's estimation, only one of them (Jill Stevens, the doctor) had even the slightest glimmer of *maybe* a *little* bit of power. But then said no, that feeling in her belly could just be a hunger pang.

Despite Erin's apparent potential, the rest of the Digby blood appeared to have been diluted too far over the past century. Autumn told me that witches marrying strangers had that effect. (*Marrying strangers* sounded ridiculous, but that was how she put it.) Nobody knew for sure how the craft was passed down, there being no studies on the subject. Sometimes it might show up a few generations on, even without a lot of witch blood. Sometimes it went the other way, and somebody who should've been a witch turned out not to be. But usually it worked like any other trait, which was why marrying strangers was discouraged. I guessed the Bryd Hollow strangers were just too enticing for the Bryd Hollow witches to resist.

All of that made me wonder about Molly's husband, Chester Towe. Autumn agreed that for Molly's power to carry down enough generations to reach Erin, her husband was likely a witch too. And if tracing his line failed, Erin's other grandparents and great-grandparents were worth checking out.

"Tracking down the witch blood was a solid idea,"

Autumn said as we piled into my car to head back to Tybryd. "The fact that it didn't work out with Erin just means we'll have to come back another time and keep looking."

I wasn't sure how that was going to work; by tomorrow, the whole town would know that I'd brought three weirdos into Yore to accost Erin Radcliffe. So much for not embarrassing myself. The chances of anybody being willing to talk to the four of us together seemed slim now. But maybe we'd have better luck if we brought Percy with us. Adoring Percy was practically a local hobby, like the book club.

"Can Gravy hang out at the daycare a while longer?" Autumn asked as we approached Tybryd's grand front entrance. The famous bloodred rhododendrons that lined the drive wouldn't bloom for another three months or so, but it was still an impressive sight, with the ferris wheel looming over the gardens and grounds.

I loved this place fiercely. I sure would've liked to help bring justice to the person who'd put a fresh black mark by its name when they killed a defenseless woman in her room.

Holly stuck her head between the front seats. "Minerva?" she prompted.

"Sorry. Wool gathering. Of course, Gravy can stay as long as you want. I'll be working until ten, since I'm going in so late."

"Good." Holly sat back again. "Because I want to have a drink or two at the bar before we have dinner. I'm still full anyway." We'd stopped on our way back from the hospital—for donuts. It wasn't exactly the fuel of champions, but I guessed it had done the trick.

"Do you have to go in right away?" Autumn asked. "You could probably use a drink yourself."

"I wish." I pulled up to the curb to drop them off. "But no, Ned's been covering for me most of the day. I have to go. But I'd love to take you guys to breakfast tomorrow morning, if I could." We agreed it was a date, and parted ways.

Despite Autumn's reassurances that we would keep trying, I felt dejected as I parked in Tailbryd's lot. It seemed Ruby had been right: there really weren't all that many witches in Bryd Hollow. We'd seen plenty of townsfolk in passing, in the course of observing our suspects, and Ivy still hadn't found a single one.

What if there weren't any at all?

Apart from the fact that I had no idea how we would find Barbara's killer if that proved to be the case, I found myself disappointed by the possibility. All the history in Bryd Hollow already felt a little bit magical—I swore I could feel the ghosts of the past, sometimes—and I kind of liked the idea of having magic around me.

Not that I'd let Percy hear me spouting such whimsical nonsense. He'd probably declare me unfit to mother his children.

Taren and Ned were behind the front desk when I walked in. I peeked into the office and, upon finding Plant's bed empty, was informed he was out playing with Gravy and a couple other little dogs.

"Gravy tends to yap when I separate them, so I've been keeping them together," Ned said.

"Good idea." Plant was always good with the little ones anyway. "They can rest up here together when they come inside. Gravy will be here another couple of hours, I would guess." I wheeled my chair out of the office, since Ned and Taren were occupying the two already at the desk, and sank into it with a deep sigh.

"Bad day?" Ned asked.

I leaned my head back and rubbed my forehead. "Foiled by Ruby Walker and *Camelot*."

Ned chuckled. "Camelot the place, or *Camelot* the musical?"

"The musical." My phone vibrated. I took it out of my pocket, expecting a message from Percy teasing me for narrowly evading arrest and bringing the judgment of the town down upon me. I'd texted him the summary a couple of hours before, and hadn't heard back yet.

But it was a message from Jane-Ann Weaver—and it had three attachments. She'd sent along the pictures of Harry Cotswold I'd asked for.

"I guess it could've been worse," said Ned. "It could've been *Grease*."

"I love *Grease*!" Taren protested.

Ned snickered. "You would."

She huffed. "What is that supposed to mean?"

Personally, I didn't mind *Grease*, but I didn't have much to say on the subject either. I started to tune them out a little as I opened one of the photos and zoomed in on an early-twentieth-century man and his wife, dressed up for something formal.

"I've never seen *Camelot*," Taren said. "Is it good?"

"Is it *good*?" Ned echoed. "It's got everything.

Knights, sword fights, magic, tragic love. The only thing it's really missing is a dog. Archimedes the owl is no substitute for a dog."

Taren started promising him she'd rent the movie sometime soon, but I'd gone from half listening to not listening at all. Something about this picture ...

I sat up straighter. Squinted at it. Zoomed in some more. Zoomed out. Zoomed in again.

Then realized what it was that had struck me.

I bolted out of my chair and dragged it back toward the office. "Guys, I need a ... I'll be back. I have to check something."

I kicked the office door behind me, half closing it, and sat down in front of my computer. The Baird family photos were all on a shared drive, where Mrs. B could access them too. Thankfully, I'd organized them well, with plenty of tags and keywords for searching.

I typed in *Emily*, *ball*, *opera*, and *party*. I knew it wasn't the first Baird ball in 1913, because I knew that picture well enough to visualize it from memory, down to pretty much every detail. But apart from that, I wasn't sure exactly what I was looking for.

But I would know it when I saw it.

Okay, I would know it the second time I saw it. I passed it over once, because I was looking for something more formal. But I found it when I clicked through the search results for the second time: Emily and Alistair in the summer of 1912, at a Newport garden party. Emily was wearing a pearl necklace with a single dark gem at the center. Ruby or emerald at my guess, but I couldn't tell in black and white. Single, but large, falling in a teardrop

179

from the pearls and surrounded by smaller stones. I'd have called it way too much for daytime, but who was I to judge.

It was the same necklace Harry Cotswold's wife was wearing in a photograph taken in … I grabbed my phone and pulled up Jane-Ann's message again, to double check I had the year right.

I did. Jane-Ann said that photograph had been taken in 1915.

It was exactly the same. I was certain of it. The same gem. The same necklace. He hadn't even bothered to change the setting.

And how else would Harry Cotswold's wife have come by Emily Baird's necklace, other than by the extortion of Tilly Mistmantle, that summer when she'd stolen some jewelry from Tybryd and then disappeared?

I'd found Tilly's mysterious stranger. I'd found her blackmailer.

I'd found her killer.

Chapter Eighteen

I OPENED the photograph of the midsummer party for one more lingering look. I still didn't know for sure which of the women we'd narrowed it down to was Tilly, posing as Edith.

"But I know who killed you," I said to the face I still thought most likely. She had Lester's jawline. "That'll just have to be enough for you to rest easy."

I had to say, it was a little anticlimactic, solving a hundred-and-twenty-year-old murder. Not nearly as satisfying as solving a modern one, even if there was less chance of a person getting shot.

At first it was great; I had that moment of exultation you get when you've solved a particularly confounding carriwitchet. I'd done it! I'd gotten to the bottom of it!

But then came the obvious response:

And?

So what?

For one thing, I could not—could *never*—be truly sure I had solved it. It all fit, it all made sense, and the evidence-from-afar, as far as I was concerned, was overwhelming. But I couldn't prove it, could I? I doubted I could get a team of forensic experts to work the case, even if there was any forensic evidence to be found all these years later, which let's face it, there wasn't.

I could close the case in my mind, and probably in the minds of the few other people who cared what had happened to Matilda Mistmantle. But I couldn't close it officially. I couldn't close it beyond all doubt. Which meant it would always be half open.

I could never see Tilly's murderer brought to justice.

And I could say the same about Edith Baird's murder. In many ways that felt worse; it was Edith I'd felt that spark of kinship with, when I first heard her story. Edith who'd captured my imagination and become, briefly, my obsession. Edith whose final moments on a hopeless April night I could never trace.

Could she rest easy now, too, in the cold depths to which she'd been so unceremoniously consigned? Maybe; maybe she had been resting easy since the summer of 1913. Justice had already been served, where she was concerned. Tilly had paid the price for that crime. Or so it seemed.

Almost as bad as the lack of hard proof of my triumph was the fact that there was nobody to tell about it. I was sitting in the office at Tailbryd, and not even my dog was here. What good was being such a fizzing detective, if I couldn't even brag?

I composed a quick email to Jane-Ann, summarizing what I'd found and attaching the picture of Emily wearing her necklace. Jane-Ann could decide for herself how to use that information, and whether she wanted to tell her cousin. If she decided not to, that was fine with me. Harry was long gone, beyond any judgment but the final one. Besmirching his name now wouldn't help anybody, and might cause a ninety-three-year-old woman some pointless pain.

See what I mean? Anticlimactic.

I texted Percy, but Chicago was an hour behind me, and he was probably still busy with the soap people. I tried Mrs. B next, but who knew what she was doing. Not looking at her phone, that was what.

Autumn! Autumn would care, surely. I texted her that I knew who'd killed Tilly Mistmantle, and received an almost immediate response back, with several satisfying exclamation points.

But the conversation petered out after that. *Ugh*, she said, *We're still at the bar, and Holly is getting up on stage to sing.*

Is that bad? I asked.

It is when it's not karaoke night.

Oops. I laughed.

"What's so funny?" Ned came in, followed by the sound of heavy panting that preceded one very large and one very small dog who were equals, it seemed, in their exhaustion.

Plant barely gave me a poke with his nose on his way by, before throwing himself down on his bed. Gravy didn't even look my way, just curled up next to Plant and immediately closed his eyes.

"Well, hello to you too, guys."

"They've had a long day," Ned said.

"Looks like it." *I'll fill you in on the rest tomorrow*, I typed to Autumn at the same time.

"Do you have any more sticky notes?" Ned asked. "We're out in front."

"Yeah, I've got some here." I opened my bottom desk drawer while I read Autumn's reply: *And I assume you'll be showing off your Marvelous Mistmantle Murder Solving Magic to Ruby?*

For sure. Ruby probably wouldn't do anything, other than add a note to the thin case file of the skeleton who'd gone from Jane Doe to Edith Baird and back again. But after our conversation today, I had a feeling she would believe me, at least. I could take some satisfaction in that.

I looked back at Ned. "I can't find them in here." I set down my phone and rummaged harder through the office supplies. I'd *just bought* some sticky notes. Where had I put them?

"Hello?" a voice called from out front. "I'm looking for a Minerva?"

I backed up my chair—nearly running over Ned—and craned my neck to see a tall man dressed in all black standing at the desk. "Where's Taren?" I whispered.

"Cleaning out the kennels."

Well, the guest had asked for me anyway. I hopped out of my chair and told Ned to check the middle drawer instead. "I'm Minerva," I said as I walked out of the office. "How can I help you?"

Up close, I saw he was also wearing black eyeliner to go with his black turtleneck and black slacks. "Sajani over in Events told me I could come and talk to you. I need to make some special arrangements for a wedding."

"What sort of special arrangements?"

"There's a separate wedding party, you know in addition to the regular kind of bridesmaids and groomsmen, that's everyone's pets. Dogs and cats, about twelve of them."

"How cute!" A little weird, but sure, cute.

He asked whether we had one giant kennel that would accommodate this entire party while the humans were eating dinner, and was very disappointed to hear we did not. He didn't want them separated into different crates, even if they were in the same room. It was a *wedding*, after all. It was all about family and *togetherness*. That last bit was delivered in the tone of a man who thought he was very smart, talking to a woman he thought was very not-smart.

I wondered whether Sajani had failed to forewarn me about this one as some sort of practical joke.

"We have outdoor play yards," I offered. "Or you could just have the reception outdoors, then they could stay with you."

"It'll be *July*," he said with a huff. "We can't be outside!"

Surely Ned must have found the sticky notes by now. He was just hiding in there so he wouldn't have to help deal with this guy.

Hey, I thought, as the guest droned on about the importance of the pets not getting their outfits "soiled" while they were here, *Ned. Ned will be impressed with my detective skills. I can tell him all about Tilly as soon as I get rid of the Condescending Goth.* It wouldn't be as fun as telling Percy or Autumn, but Ned would have to at least pretend to be interested, on account of me being his boss.

He probably was at least a little genuinely interested, anyway. He was sort of involved; he'd been here all day, when the bones were found. In fact, he was one of the first people to see them. And he'd come to Baird House to pick up Tabitha, so maybe he even saw the spellb—

Odsbodikins!

I coughed into my fist to cover a gasp.

I'd gotten a little nagging feeling, during that half conversation with Ned and Taren while I was looking at Jane-Ann's email. That feeling you get when something is off, but you're too distracted to see it out of more than the corner of your eye. At the time, I'd lumped it in with the other nagging feeling that came from trying to pinpoint what was wrong in Harry's photo. My mind was back in 1913.

But now my mind was here—in the present, at least, if not with this insufferable guest—and that feeling came rushing back at me. Along with the feeling I should've paid a lot better attention to it the first time.

Because I'd just realized its cause. It was only a little thing. A meaningless thing, really. But there were other little things, too.

Was it possible that added together, they came to one big thing?

OdsBODikins!

Get it together, Minerva. No dangerous situations, remember? Act normal until you can get some backup in here.

"Well, there may be a few options for us," I told the

guest, hoping my voice didn't falter. "I can look into tenting one of the play yards. We also have an indoor play room that we use when the weather is inclement, but that would only work if we didn't need it for any other dogs in addition to your party."

By his scandalized face, I might have suggested murdering his four-legged wedding party and serving them as appetizers. "Oh, I don't want any strange dogs in with them! I'm sure if your superiors put their heads together, they can come up with something better than that."

My heart was pounding, and my hands were starting to shake. I needed to get rid of this ratbag, and fast. Thankfully, his ratbagginess had just given me an opening. As far as dog daycare went, I was the end of the line, but it didn't seem like Sajani had told him that. "That's a great idea! If you give me your contact information, I'll talk to my boss and look into some things, and put together a proposal for you with a few options. Then you can choose what best suits your needs."

To my very great relief, he agreed. As soon as he left, I reached into my back pocket for my phone. Who to text first? Ruby, or Autumn?

Well, neither, because my phone wasn't there. I must have left it on my desk. I whirled around—and found Ned leaning against the closed office door.

"How long have you been standing there?" I asked, in the best approximation of *bright and breezy* I could manage.

"A bit."

I plastered on what was probably a ridiculous smile.

"That guy was something, huh? Here, let me in there a sec, I'm just going to grab my phone and—"

"And show off your marvelous Mistmantle-murder-solving magic to Ruby Walker?" Ned shook his head and stepped forward, careful to keep himself between me and the door. Which also kept him between me and my phone—and my dog.

Then he pulled a knife out of his pocket, and snapped it open.

Chapter Nineteen

HIGHLIGHT/LOWLIGHT of being held captive at knife point by Ned Phelps: The highlight was, at least it wasn't a gun. I had a bit of a phobia of guns. Does it count as a phobia, if it's not an irrational fear? Because I had every reason to be afraid of guns. Lots of people who'd taken more than one bullet on more than one occasion would be.

But this wasn't a gun. Just a knife.

"Just" a knife. Ha.

Everything else was lowlight, really.

"Stay where you are," Ned said.

That was fine by me. I was a couple steps away from him—just out of stabbing distance, I hoped.

He jerked his head back toward the office door he was still blocking. "I've got your dog in there. I'd rather not, but I will gut him if I have to, Min, don't test me."

I gave him a small nod, but didn't say anything. Mainly because I hadn't yet decided what to say. I was taking stock of my situation as quickly as I could, but I wasn't great under the dog-hostage-slash-mortal-peril kind of pressure.

Think. Stay calm. It's not like it's a gun. Think.

There was no point in playing innocent and asking what this was all about. He'd obviously seen some of my text exchange with Autumn while he was lingering behind me waiting for his sticky notes. Stupid small office. But not enough of it to realize we were talking about the last Mistmantle murder, not the current one.

Not the one he'd committed.

The *just a knife* was one of those spring-loaded ones where the blade flipped out the side, like my father always carried. Small enough to clip inside a front pocket (of men's pants, anyway), but you couldn't let the efficient size fool you into thinking they were just for opening packages. Dad had once accidentally sliced open his thigh, and it was so bad my mother had to rush him to the emergency room, lecturing him the whole way for being clumsy and bleeding all over her car and almost— but not completely, if he knew what was good for him —dying.

So *could* Ned gut Plant with that thing? (The word *gut* made me physically ill. I kind of wanted to stab Ned just for using it.) I wasn't sure I liked anybody's odds in close combat with Plant; that boy had his own sharp and pointy parts. If Ned went into the office, I would just call out a command loudly enough to wake the napping dogs. Plant had some guard dog training. He didn't have a word for attack, but he knew *hold* perfectly well.

Except Ned was his buddy. Ned wasn't a threat. If commanded to hold Ned, he would probably think it was a training session, which for Plant was synonymous with treat session. He'd probably hold for all of five seconds before he trotted up to Ned demanding his reward. At which point he'd get stabbed instead.

All right, then if Ned got anywhere near my dog, I'd just have to attack him myself. Him stabbing me and me screaming in pain would tip Plant off that this wasn't playtime. Then it would be two against one, and surely Team Biggs could take Ned down. This was *Ned* we were talking about. Mild-mannered, baby-faced Ned. We were *way* tougher than Ned.

But could we do it without either of us getting filleted like a fish first?

I wasn't loving the way all these scenarios ended with Plant getting stabbed. And there was Gravy to think of. I couldn't exactly let him get stabbed, either. Although he was a much smaller target, and probably harder to catch.

It took me five, maybe ten seconds after Ned said the words *don't test me* to play all of this out and decide the man had a point: I'd rather not test it. I would if I had to, but I'd really rather find another way out of this, if I could.

Talking, then. Make him see reason. "What are you going to do, Ned? Stab me right here in the lobby? Taren is here."

"Taren is cleaning the kennels, it'll probably take her an hour. You know how slow she is. And she's got her headphones on."

"And what if a guest comes in to drop off or pick up? I guess you could lock the doors?" I asked hopefully.

That would require him to move away from the office door.

But Ned wasn't about to give up his hostages. "I'm not moving and neither are you. If you scream or run for the doors, I'll kill the dogs. I'll do it, Min."

I did not like him calling me Min. Percy called me Min, now that his Mini Bigs phase had blessedly passed. My sister called me Min. Crazy lamp—and possibly knife —murderers did not get to call me Min.

But this seemed like a bad time to complain.

"If somebody comes in, or Taren comes back out here, act normal and don't do anything stupid," Ned went on. "You don't want anyone else getting hurt, do you?"

I tossed my arms. "How many people are you going to stab, Ned?"

He raised his chin. "As many as I have to, I guess. Believe it or not, I'm actually trained in knife fighting."

"They have classes for that kind of thing?" I kept my voice casual, like this was any other conversation while we were behind the desk and things were slow.

Which took some doing, considering how not-casual I was feeling on the inside. On the inside, I felt like somebody had just put my stomach and heart through a meat grinder, and then put them back in the wrong positions.

"Sure," said Ned. "Any martial arts place will teach you."

I tipped my chin toward the office. "You were in there for how long, while I was talking to Mansplainer McGoth? And the best plan you could come up with was *I'll stab as many people as I have to*?"

"Well what am I supposed to do? I can't just let you text Ruby!"

I shook my head at him, like he'd screwed up a reservation. "You could at least have taken the time to scroll up on my phone and read the whole text exchange."

"I tried," he said defensively. "Your lock screen came on. But I saw enough. I know who Autumn is. I saw her name on Gravy's reservation when we were printing out the guest list this morning." Ned contorted his face, like a ballplayer who'd just struck out and couldn't figure out how that last pitch had gotten by him. "I thought I made sure she didn't see me when she dropped him off."

"She didn't see you."

He frowned. "Then how did she know?"

"She doesn't know anything about you. She doesn't know you, she's never seen you, and I feel pretty comfortable presuming you've never once crossed her mind."

The frown deepened. "Then how do *you* know? I assumed she told you I was a witch, and you put the rest together."

"And that is what you get for reading a fraction of a text exchange and making assumptions! We weren't even talking about you and Barbara. We were talking about Tilly Mistmantle and Harry Cotswold."

Well what do you know, I'd gotten to brag to Ned about solving Tilly's murder, after all. It was even less satisfying than anticipated.

"No." Ned shook his head hard. "No way. Nope. You're lying."

"I can see why it's difficult to accept that you just pulled a knife on your boss, threatened her dog, and gave yourself away as a murderer for no good reason at all. But I'm afraid that's exactly what happened."

Ned shook his head again, as if I might have missed the first four denials. "It was all over your face when you turned around and saw me just then. And your smile was all weird, and your voice was like three times higher than normal. You definitely knew."

I looked heavenward and heaved a very long, very exasperated sigh. Not entirely for show, either. There was a fair amount of sincerity in that sigh. "Archimedes isn't in *Camelot*, Ned."

He blinked at me. "What?"

"Archimedes. The owl. You said he was no substitute for a dog in *Camelot*."

"Well he's not."

"No, he's definitely not, and do you know why? Because he's not even there. This is what I'm saying."

"He's not in *Camelot*?"

"Nope."

"What's he in, then?"

What did he care? I was keeping him talking largely to stall him, while I tried to think of some options here that wouldn't get me or my dog or Autumn's dog stabbed. Or Taren. Or a guest. Or anybody, really, although at the moment I wouldn't have minded so much if it were Ned who got stabbed.

But I had the oddest feeling that Ned was stalling me right back. Why? What did he have to gain from that? Every second we spent talking added to the not insignificant risk that somebody would walk in on us.

Maybe he was stalling to give himself time to come

up with a better plan, same as I was. He couldn't *want* to stab me. He was a sweet kid, when he wasn't murdering little old ladies. We were friends. And even if that was all an act, and he was actually harboring a secret hatred of me, he definitely didn't want to stab any dogs. Nobody could fake loving dogs. Dogs could tell.

It didn't really matter. If he wanted to stall, let him. In this one thing, we were in accord.

"He's in *The Sword in the Stone*," I said. "The animated thing. But don't feel too bad about getting them confused, they're both based on *The Once and Future King*."

"And that's your whole problem? You decided I'm a murderer because Archimedes isn't in *Camelot*?" Ned huffed. "That is the stupidest thing I've ever heard."

"Oh come on, I doubt that. You're doing something even stupider right now."

"You just told me not to feel bad about getting them confused! It was an honest mistake!"

"It might have been, if your cousin had played somebody else. But you specifically said he was Merlin."

"So?"

"So, Archimedes is *Merlin's* owl. You would've noticed whether or not there was an owl on your own cousin's shoulder the whole play." I pointed at him. "Unless you weren't really there. Unless you lied to Ruby about where you were when Barbara died. And only guilty people need to lie about their alibis."

"Nope, I stand by my ruling. That is definitely the stupidest thing I've ever heard."

"Yeah well, Ruby tells me it's usually a stupid thing

that gets you caught. And everything else fits. You were one of the few people who saw all of Tilly Mistmantle's things firsthand. Maybe you didn't know at the time that she was Tilly Mistmantle, but—"

I snapped my fingers, realizing something. "But you were out front here, when I was in the office telling Percy and Mrs. B that Edith Baird was actually Tilly. You probably heard the whole story."

"That was after Barbara was killed, though."

"So you did hear it." I waved all that away. "But you're right, it doesn't matter. The point is, you recognized the Mistmantle family emblem. You knew what those things were."

"A lot of people would've known what those things were."

"But not many of them live in Bryd Hollow. Turns out we're kind of short on witches here, did you know that?"

"Ugh." Ned rolled his eyes. "Tell me about it. My family are the only ones I know of, and my mother has a cow if I date a stranger."

"Is that why you tried to convince everybody the killer was Mrs. Gochev? Because you knew if we started looking for a witch, your family would be the only ones we'd find?" And they weren't even related to Molly Towe, at least not that I'd seen. Just my luck, I guessed, hiring one of the random needles in the Bryd Hollow haystack. "Who was Mrs. Gochev, anyway?"

"Forget it. I'll never tell you who she is, and you'll never find her."

"Hope that doesn't mean you killed her."

"I don't just go around killing people!"

"But you killed Barbara." It wasn't a question, obviously, and Ned didn't deny it. He must have known there was no walking back this whole threatening me with a knife thing.

I nodded, as if he'd confirmed it out loud instead of just by doing something incredibly stupid. "We knew the killer was probably either somebody Barbara knew or somebody on staff, somebody she would let into her room. My guess is, you went back to her room on some pretense or other about the cat."

He shrugged. "I told her it was the first time we'd used the cat room, and that I'd just found some mold in it while I was cleaning it after, so I wanted to give Tabitha some Benadryl in case she was allergic."

I crossed my arms. "You told her there was *mold* in my brand new state-of-the-art facility?"

"It got her to let me in! She was a real"—Ned made an exaggerated throat-clearing noise—"*witch* about it, too."

"Did you actually give that poor cat Benadryl?"

"Yeah. She was a familiar. I wanted her sleepy, in case things got dragged out."

"And did they? Maybe you offered to buy the focus and the book, and things got out of hand? Maybe it was self-defense?" I raised my brows in hope. "Throw me a bone here, Ned. I'm ready to believe that Barbara was a bad witch."

Ready, willing, and able. Not only was there plenty of evidence that Barbara had been something of a ratbag, but it suited my present circumstances to think that Ned was not a cold-blooded killer.

But he scowled at me. "No, things didn't get out of hand. What things would there even be, to get out of hand? There were no things. You think I was going to confront her? Ask nicely?"

"Um. I guess no?"

"Of course not. She had the Mistmantle things. All their spells. She even could've been a Mistmantle witch, somehow, for all I knew. I wasn't about to take any chances with her."

"So, no argument or anything."

Bless his heart, the man actually laughed. "I waited until she bent over the bed to kiss her cat. The only thing she had time to say was that if I was standing around waiting for a tip, I could forget it. Then I whacked her on the head." Ned jabbed a finger at me to drive his point home. "And it's a good thing I did, because it turned out she *was* a Mistmantle witch. So there."

Alrighty then. So he was a cold-blooded killer.

I definitely needed to get away from him. I definitely needed to get my *dog* away from him.

I was just about resolved that I was going to have to attack him after all, when the front doors slid open, and Autumn Trelayne walked in.

"Hey, I'm pretty much Holly-and-Ivied out. I'm just going to grab Gravy and order some room ser—what is going *on* here?"

Chapter Twenty

IT WASN'T me who'd prompted Autumn to ask that question. Not wanting to get stabbed, or get her stabbed, or get either of our dogs stabbed, I'd half turned—I wasn't about to turn my back fully on Ned Phelps right now—and smiled at her like everything was normal.

But it seemed she knew things were not normal. "Your friend is a witch?" she asked.

Before I could answer, Ned had grabbed me around the shoulders and yanked me back, my back against his chest. And his knife at my throat.

So that was pretty great. I might as well have turned my back all the way, if that was the best I could do on a half turn.

"All right then," said Autumn. "Not your friend. But still a witch."

"Don't do anything stupid," Ned said to her. I did not like feeling Ned Phelps's breath on my hair.

"I wouldn't dream of it. Where is Gravy?"

I was not offended by her asking after Gravy instead

of expressing concern for my safety. It would've been my first question too, if I'd found a psycho in the lobby of the place I was boarding my dog. "He's fine."

"For now," said Ned.

"He's in the office, napping with Plant," I went on. Perfectly casually. I saw no reason to break my resolve to stay calm just because that knife had gotten a lot closer to my vital veins. Arteries? I could never remember the difference. "They're oblivious to our little situation here. They were exhausted."

I thought of Ned saying he'd given Tabitha Benadryl because he knew she was a familiar and wanted to make sure she was sleepy, in case anything went wrong. I wondered if he'd made sure Plant and Gravy played extra hard for the same reason. I hoped he hadn't given *them* Benadryl. I was still pretty sure my best hope was to get my guard dog to help me take this clown down.

It was a tricky thing to visualize, because while I knew I needed Plant's help to overpower Ned, I also needed for Plant to not get stabbed. If anybody absolutely had to get stabbed, I'd prefer Ned, but I was willing to take a wound or two myself, for Plant's sake.

Just not in the throat.

Unless Autumn could save the day with magic and the power of friendship, or something. But she'd repeatedly told me that she couldn't just fling a fireball on demand. Which I guessed was fine, since there was probably some risk of her lighting my hair on fire instead of Ned, now that he had me pinned against him with that stupid knife at my throat.

"Did you know he was a witch?" Autumn asked me.

"No, I didn't know! Don't you think I would've told you if I knew?"

"Well don't get snippy with me, he's the one with the knife."

"How did *you* know he was a witch? I thought you couldn't detect witches."

"I can't. But I know when a spell is being cast right in front of me."

"He's casting a sp—" I started to turn my head to scowl at Ned, but the point of the knife pricked at me, and I decided it would be better to stay still for the time being. "You're casting a spell?" I guessed that explained why he'd been stalling me.

"He *was* casting a spell, or trying to. But he's going to stop now, aren't you ..." Autumn looked from Ned to me, her face inquisitive.

"Ned," I provided.

"Oh! So this is Ned. He *was* your friend, so I was sort of right." She raised her hands and took a few steps forward, away from the door, but still kept the desk between us. "Let's stay calm here, Ned, and not hurt the stranger. We try to avoid that, remember? Good witch PR? I won't cast spells, you won't cast spells."

Then she added, as if it were an afterthought, "And probably you shouldn't stab her either."

Other than threatening the dogs, Ned had stayed quiet throughout our exchange, but now he let out an annoyed huff. "I was casting the spell so I wouldn't *have* to stab her. But I guess you just ruined that, so if I do stab her, you can thank yourself."

"Just out of curiosity, what kind of spell was this?" I asked.

"To make you forget everything," he said.

Autumn pursed her lips at him, like he was a student who'd been sloppy with something when he should've known better. "Even if you were burning butterbur and orange, which I notice you are not, she'd have to sleep for that to work. For a few hours, at least."

"I know that!" Ned said. "I'd have drugged her or something. I don't know. I was thinking on my feet."

"Not very well," I muttered.

He pinched my shoulder. "Nobody asked you."

"She's not wrong, though. It was a weak spell." Autumn was fidgeting with a leather cord that disappeared below her collar, and I belatedly remembered the protection charms Ivy had made us. I was still wearing mine, too.

Either Ivy was very bad at magic, or magic definitely was not real.

Unless that wasn't her protection charm Autumn was fidgeting with. I hadn't actually seen her put hers on. I remembered her fingers drifting to her throat the day we met her at Holly Tree Lane. I'd wondered then whether she had a focus of her own.

Had she lied just now, about not casting any spells? Did she think she could do it without Ned being able to tell?

And if she was lying, and was casting a spell, just how *much* time did spells take? And could a focus speed them up at all?

"Did you feel anything?" she asked me. "Any fuzziness in your head? Memory confusion? Sudden unexplained doubts?"

"Nope, not a thing," I said. "I had no idea."

"See? Weak spell." She gave Ned a pitying look. "You're not a very good witch, are you?"

"Oh, he's definitely a bad witch." I was probably risking another pinch with my snark, but I couldn't help it. I was getting crabby. As anybody in my situation would.

I heard stirring in the office, followed by an inquisitive yap. Maybe Gravy was questioning Ned's magic skills, too.

Ned sighed. "Did you just call to your familiar?"

"Of course not," said Autumn. "He probably just heard my voice."

As if in confirmation, Gravy yapped twice more.

"Plant might be used to being closed in there while you're out here," she said, "but Gravy's not."

"Go on then, shut him up," said Ned.

"Grave, quiet," Autumn called. "Hold your horses a minute."

He quieted, but evidently he'd already woken up Plant, because I heard the sound of a big paw scratching at the office door. Autumn wasn't entirely right; Plant was used to being in there, but he wasn't used to the door being closed unless I was in there with him.

Was there some way to get that door open? Even if I disregarded the knife at my throat, I couldn't reach the knob from where I was. I'd have to find a way to back up.

"Is that why you stole the spellbook?" I asked.

"Because you're not very good at spells, and were hoping to take advantage of some of that Mistmantle skill?"

Ned scoffed. "You thought I stole that book to *use* it? What kind of person do you take me for?"

"Well, not a very good one, Ned! Look around!"

I guessed that had come out a little too loud; Gravy yapped again, and Plant joined him with a whine and a soft *woof* of his own.

Ned gave me a jerk, his nails digging into me. At least that was better than the knife. "Calm down. Pretty sure you don't want to get those dogs involved."

Pretty sure I do, Ned.

"Plant, settle," I called. *For now.* "Be there in a minute."

"So you didn't take the book to use it." Autumn's tone was a lot more abrupt than it had been a minute ago. "Did you sell it?"

"Of course I didn't sell it!" Ned still sounded offended that we thought he was that kind of guy. "Mistmantle magic shouldn't exist in the world. Those were dark spells. *Evil* spells. I burned the book the second I got home."

"And the focus?" Autumn asked. "There'd be no need to destroy that. Its power would've been raw, not directed or specific. Not good or evil."

Plant scratched at the door again. He was not settling. Maybe I'd sounded too tense. Gravy whined, then let out a long warbling sound I could only describe as a yodel.

"Would you *shut them up*!" Ned snapped. "And forget about the focus. You'll never find it."

"Kind of like Mrs. Gochev?" I asked. He'd used almost those same words about her.

Plant snuffled under the door, but he didn't bark. And despite her claims at having no telepathic connection to her familiar, maybe Autumn had given Gravy some silent command, because he was quiet again, too.

"I'm surprised you didn't try to finish off the Mistmantle line, while you were at it," said Autumn. "Or do you have my cousin's gift for recognizing witches? Did you realize Kim had no power?"

"Kim." Ned dismissed her with a snort. "She had nothing at all. I killed the last real Mistmantle witch. You're welcome, by the way."

I guessed this would be a bad time to tell him about Kim's son John.

Autumn started to say something else, but the doorway that led to the kennels opened and Taren came through, headphones still in, singing to herself. She started to say something to Ned, then caught a glimpse of the knife just as he was trying to pull it out of sight.

Which required him to pull it away from my neck.

And then a lot of things happened at once, or in such close sequence as to feel that way.

Taren screamed. Plant and Gravy immediately went ballistic in response. By the sound of it, Plant threw himself at the door. Ned's head started swiveling in several directions, as if he didn't know what his priority ought to be. *(Not stabbing me, Ned.)*

He was clearly panicking. Poor guy, he wasn't a super experienced hostage taker. And now he had three women in three different locations to contend with, one of them a witch, in addition to two practically rabid dogs and unlocked front doors.

It was as much distraction as I was likely to get. So I decided it was all I needed.

His arm was still around me, but he'd loosened his grip when he tried to hide the knife. I gave his forearm a good hard bite to loosen it a little more. Then I dropped to the floor.

My intention had been to yank on his ankles to knock him down. It made sense in my head. In reality, his ankles would not budge. I'd done a fizzing job of getting his attention, though. I rolled away as he swung the knife.

I can't explain what happened next. Mainly because I was on the floor, rolling, and didn't see it. But I heard it: the office door banging against the wall behind it. Shame Ned wasn't on that side, it would've hit him right in the face.

Instead what hit him in the face was a very large, very angry dog. So that settled the question of whether Plant could tell if I was being attacked for real, even by a friend.

I yelped, terrified my dog was going to get stabbed, and scrambled to my feet. I had to get that knife away from Ned, while Plant occupied him with trying to defend his jugular. (Vein, right? I was pretty sure that one was a vein.)

But by the time I got up, it was already pretty much over. Ned crashed to the floor, Plant on top of him, and let out a hollow wheeze. He'd been too busy coming after me, and Plant had come at him too fast, too unexpect-

THE GUEST IS HISTORY

edly; he hadn't managed to stab Plant before Plant tackled him.

And now that he'd had the wind knocked out of him, he would never get the chance. All that was left for me to do was stomp on Ned's hand as hard as I could, then kick the knife away as his fingers released it.

I gave him a nice kick in the side too, for good measure. Ratbag.

"Plant, hold," I panted.

I didn't have to tell him twice.

Chapter Twenty-One

WHEN YOU'RE A LITTLE KID, magic is simply a given. Of course there are worlds at the backs of wardrobes. Of course talking bears in red hats eat donuts at Paddington Station. Of course nannies float down to your doorstep by umbrella, and owls deliver the mail. You never question any of this. It's just the world.

And then the world slowly begins to shrink. It starts with Santa, and it gets worse from there. They call this *growing up*.

I can't quite say whether Autumn Trelayne made me believe in magic again. But she definitely made me miss it.

And I told Percy so, as soon as he got back from Chicago. Which was on the first flight he could get after he heard what happened, and if that hadn't been soon enough, he probably would've chartered a private plane, poor man. Of course he was beside himself at not having been there when his damsel was in distress. Percy Baird was a white knight by nature. He loved nothing more than saving people—and feared nothing more than failing to.

He caught me at my apartment shortly after I got back from having breakfast with the Trelaynes. Holly and Ivy were just as upset as Percy over missing all the excitement the night before, and had loudly complained all the way through their pancakes that *nothing ever* happened to them, while *everything always* happened to Autumn.

I was fairly certain Ned's breakfast had been a lot less pleasant, on account of his being in jail. Ruby was also pondering charging several members of his family, immediate and extended, who'd told her ("To my *face!*" as she'd told me) that he was at *Camelot* the night of the murder. It seemed the Phelps witches were all united in their conviction that a Mistmantle witch should not be suffered to live.

Neither the spellbook nor the focus had been recovered as yet. Presumably the former was in ashes. Possibly the latter was off somewhere with the mysterious Mrs. Gochev, never to be seen again. I didn't really care, to tell you the truth. Let Autumn worry about her artifacts. I'd solved two murders in one day, and seen justice served to the only one of the murderers it could be served to, and that was good enough for me.

I assured Percy that Plant and I had managed just fine without him, but stopped short of the words *we didn't need you*. Not only because they would have hurt Percy's feelings. Somehow they didn't ring quite true.

Then I sat him down on my couch, and recounted the tale of Plant miraculously growing opposable thumbs and opening the office door to save the day. All by himself, while Autumn Trelayne stood a few feet away, definitely not casting a spell.

"And did she acknowledge that she was definitely not casting a spell?" he asked.

I sighed. "She was coy about it. I assume just to torture me."

"Well, I'd have said faulty latch on the door, myself," said Percy. But for once there wasn't the slightest note of teasing in his voice. He took my hands, running his thumbs over my knuckles. "But if you believe she opened that door with some kind of spell, then I believe you."

Odsbodikins. I guessed being hundreds of miles away while Ned Phelps held a knife to my throat really had freaked him out. "I wouldn't say I *believe*-believe it. More that I wouldn't mind being open to the possibility that something happened that I can't explain." I squeezed his hands. "It makes the world a little more interesting, don't you think?"

The dimples peeked out. "I don't tend to have a problem with the world being boring. Not with you around."

"I do have a habit of attracting murderers, don't I?"

"Among others." He kissed me. "I love you, Min."

"I love you too."

He shook his head. "That's not what I'm ... I don't mean it in the usual, toss the words out before you end the phone call kind of way."

Oh. My belly fluttered. "Okay. I love you too."

"If Ned had ... and I wasn't ..." He swallowed and looked down at our still-clasped hands like studying them was a crucial task. "I can't imagine a future without you." His voice grew softer. "I can't imagine having a family with anybody else."

My smile was wobbly with the effort of trying not to cry. "Even if I'm a crackpot who raises your kids to be crackpots?"

"Even if."

"Okay. Then maybe we should have a family."

"Minerva Biggs." Percy widened his eyes and pressed his hand to his chest in an uncanny—and I hoped unconscious, given the moment—imitation of his mother. "Did you just propose marriage to me?"

"Certainly not!"

Nor would I ever. Percy was an old-fashioned guy. Like, straight out of a black-and-white movie old-fashioned. He'd probably been dreaming of going down on one knee since he was a boy, the way girls dreamed of their weddings. I wouldn't have robbed him of his moment for the world.

"Good." He stood.

"Wait." I tugged at his hand. "What do you mean, *good*?"

"Can't have you stealing my thunder."

And then, yep, he dropped to one knee. It was a good thing Plant was napping in the bedroom. He definitely would have interpreted Percy on the floor as an invitation to play, and tackled him.

"Minerva Biggs, will you do me the very great honor of becoming my wife?"

See? Old-fashioned.

I blinked away my tears long enough to catch a glimpse of the ring in his hand: not a diamond, but an emerald. It was an antique, of course, and a Baird family heirloom, because Percy knew the quickest way to my heart was through the past.

I found out later he'd been carrying it around for weeks, trying to find the right moment. He'd thought maybe Valentine's Day, but we hadn't even seen each other that day. He was working late, and I was on my couch into the wee hours, pushing taffy wrappers and Plant's head off my keyboard, trying to piece together the lives of two long-gone women I could never truly know.

Magic. The whole truth about Tilly Mistmantle. What exactly happened to Edith Cotswold Baird in the early hours of April 15, 1912. The soundness of the latch on Tailbryd's office door. There were a lot of things I would never know.

But I knew enough to say yes to Percy Baird.

Dear Reader

Thank you for reading *The Guest is History*. I hope you enjoyed it!

If you'd like to know when I've got a new book, be sure to sign up for my newsletter at cordeliarook.com. You'll find my email address there as well; I love to hear from readers!

Your honest ratings and reviews help other readers choose books. I hope you'll consider giving your opinion at your online retailer.

Minervaisms

butter upon bacon: even more of a good thing; over the top; an extravagance

carriwitchet: a befuddling question; a puzzle

fizzing: excellent; impressive

hornswaggle: a con; a willful deception

nanty-nark: have great fun; party

odsbodikins: an all-purpose expression of dismay, surprise, or irritation

pantry politicking: gossiping among the household, staff, or servants

podsnappery: a refusal to recognize the unpleasant; complacency

ratbag: a jerk; a sleazy person

vazey: airheaded; insipid

Made in United States
North Haven, CT
04 May 2023

36212680R10136